The Red Feathers

The Red Feathers

T. G. Roberts

Introduction by Martin Ware
General Editor: Malcolm Ross

New Canadian Library No. 127

McClelland and Stewart Limited

The Canadian Publishers
McClelland and Stewart Limited
25 Hollinger Road, Toronto

Printed and bound in Canada

CONTENTS

CONTENTS

Introduction

To introduce Theodore Roberts' *The Red Feathers* is to invite you to enter an imaginary world that closely resembles that of the epic romance, but an unusual one even in this respect. For *The Red Feathers* is a romance of an entirely original kind, one set in the Canadian Maritimes, and drawing on Canadian Indian mythic patterns. There can be few, if any, imaginative parallels in the range of North American literature with the energy of this adaptation of romance to a North American setting and ambience.

The strange unpredictable world of *The Red Feathers* will surely be an unfamiliar world to the contemporary reader for two obvious reasons. The first is that we have for a long time allowed ourselves to be swayed by a vogue of naturalistic realism (one soon due for an eclipse) that has imposed tight reins on our imaginative freedom. The second is that the reader is likely to know of few Canadian writers who have indulged their fantasy and succeeded in creating a self-contained imaginative world, one consistent to its own inner laws, that is rooted in a very old North American tradition. We have allowed ourselves to be so encircled by realism that we have tended to forget the few Canadian romances of excellence that we do possess.

Theodore Roberts has for too long been a forgotten author. The reasons for this are easy enough to understand. Born in New Brunswick in 1877, he was too young to have been carried on the crest of the first wave of Canadian romanticism, the one that carried his brother, Charles, with Carman, Lampman and D.C. Scott to prominence. He was too old to have been possessed by the mood of naturalistic rebelliousness (sometimes cynicism) which was endemic among the young modernists who began to make their reputations after the catastrophe of the First World War. As A. G. Bailey has suggested, Roberts was a writer who reached literary maturity during the Edwardian lull in general Canadian literary activity, and was just hitting his stride as a writer when the disaster of war struck in 1914. His best work was written during the first ten or fifteen years of the century, but the coming of war brought so sharp a reaction, so profound a change in taste, at least among younger writers, that the best of his work never received its due measure of appreciation and recognition. The modernists in their aggressive determination to clean the slate had little patience with any of the work produced in the vigorous flush of romantic optimism, and were scarcely prepared to accept such work, even on its own merits.

The time has come to reclaim *The Red Feathers* as a work of genuine imaginative power and originality, one which deserves its place in the corpus of Canadian literature. For *The Red Feathers* (published in 1907) is not simply a book for its own Edwardian time. In its energy and verve, its gentle humour and wild slapstick, its freshness and its grace, and especially in its originality and imaginative inventiveness, it is a book which deserves more lasting recognition. The shelves of Canadian literature are filled with works of realism; by contrast, works of fantasy and romance – works in which the author can give his poetic imagination full scope – are far rarer. Roberts is as much a poet as a prose writer in his *Red Feathers*. His approach calls to mind nothing so much as Sir Philip Sidney's characterization of the poet as he who "goeth hand in hand with nature, not enclosed within the narrow warrant of her gifts, but freely ranging within the zodiac of his own wit." One of the hallmarks of Roberts' work is the pleasure that he takes in imaginative flight for its own sake, but this pleasure is balanced by a gentle penetration into character and motive which is unusual in works of fantasy and romance. This aspect of his work distinguishes it from that of one of the few Canadians who has had a comparable imagination, James De Mille. De Mille's *Strange Manuscript Found in a Copper Cylinder* is one of the few Canadian books that can appropriately be set beside *The Red Feathers*, but it is much more Utopian (and thus also anti-Utopian), much more a book concerned with ideas for their own sake, than Roberts' more human and more rounded story.

Nonetheless; despite its concern with character *The Red Feathers* is a romance rather than a novel. It is set in a scarcely imaginable time when a race of whom we know tantalisingly little, the Beothuks (long since extinct), roamed the stretches of Newfoundland from the source of the Exploits River to the furthest reaches of Notre Dame Bay. Our very historical ignorance thus allows the author life-giving freedom. The theme of Roberts' book concerns the extraordinary and mysterious events that surround the titanic struggle for two little feathers. And, as is appropriate in a romance, the plot culminates in the unpredictable attempts of the hero (a baby when the book opens) to achieve his quest, and, if he can, his destiny.

The story is epic in the sense that the struggle widens to involve virtually all the inhabitants of Newfoundland (by my count at least five races are involved), that its action spans the life of a generation, that it involves the creation or destruction of a civilisation, and that its action moves in more senses than one from the icy poles to the tropics (Newfoundland lies almost exactly halfway between).

In seeking the main elements of his story, Roberts has turned to a most unusual source. He has turned (as the writer of romance almost invariably does) to the mythic tradition closest at hand, not to a commonly used European mythic tradition, but to the Micmac tradition of Nova Scotia. The crucial elements of *The Red Feathers* can be traced in the series of legends and fables, adventures and poems gathered in such collections as Silas Rand's *Legends of the Micmacs* (1893). One can discover here the mightiest and wisest of magicians, the strange Glooscap with his powers of transformation and flight, or malicious shamans who delight in tormenting their victims; one can find in these legends a widespread belief in the importance of the influence of dreams, especially on those reaching the age of initiation and responsibility; and one can enjoy here the tales of terrible cannibalistic Kookwes or giants. These elements provide the raw material of Roberts' art (in the same way that the Greek legends provided the raw material of the Greek dramatists). Roberts has transformed them for his own purposes in an entirely individual brew, one which leaves the Micmac spirit untouched but has a special flavour of its own.

What then is the approximate recipe according to which Roberts has concocted his brew? The prevailing passion for realism has tended to blind us to the need for recipes and to dull our powers of distinguishing artistic representation from its raw material in experience. It may be that the reawakening of a taste for romance involves a rediscovery of the need for literary recipes and conventions – not conventions in the esoteric academic sense, but simply a sense of generally accepted modes and means of expression that have traditionally been the basis for popular art, and provide the artist with the opportunity of varying the approved patterns in ways that bring pleasure, recognition, and new ways of perceiving.

The recipe according to which Roberts has begun his *Red Feathers* is that of the pantomime, a form until recently not very widely known in North America (except, perhaps, in Old Acadia). The action of a pantomime centres typically on a struggle between two magic forces, one represented by a benevolent wizard or fairy godmother, the other by an evil magician or devil. Generally such figures have little human individuality. Their role is simply to project the abstraction which they embody. Devils, for example, take a great pleasure in duping their human pawns, and then gloating over the fact in self-satisfied soliloquies. The action customarily revolves around the struggle between the opposed forces to achieve the happiness or work the destruction of the hero or heroine (and through them that of their community). The human figures, frequently distinguished by marked idiosyncrasies, usually project a caricature of popular types. Their power to initiate action is markedly limited by comparison with that of the magicians. It is only through purity of motive and an understanding of the applications and limitations of the available magic power that the hero (and his friends) can hope to overcome the perils that confront them, and achieve happiness of some kind.

While some such pattern can clearly be discerned in Roberts' work, to suggest that *The Red Feathers* is limited by its initiating pattern would be to do it a serious injustice. It is true, of course, that Roberts has a fine sense of the dramatic moment, one which may remind the reader of moments in pantomime. At one point in his narrative, for example, a group of friendly Indians are sitting around a campfire. One of the braves throws a log on the fire, and suddenly a shower of sparks illuminates the group, revealing a sinister stranger in a robe of bright fur. Moments of this kind – comparable with the instantaneous appearance of a devil in a puff of smoke – suggest both the popular parallels for Roberts' romance, and begin to indicate the ways in which he transforms them. For in the chambers of Roberts' imagination the pantomime form undergoes a reaction of fusion and a change of state. The conventional pattern is given a new vitality, and restored to its source in the wild energy of life.

Take, for example, one of the common features of the pantomime, the sense given of human vulnerability and weakness in the face of natural and diabolical perils. Roberts conveys this by the force of his portrayal of the Indians' total dependence on the cycle of life and of the seasons in the primeval wilds. He makes his reader constantly aware of the remorseless necessity of natural processes – of the succession of the seasons which brings with it the movement of great masses of animals, the Indians' only guarantee against starvation. It may be the melting of the snows in early spring that brings thousands on thousands of seals floating down from the North on pans of ice (magic carpets?) many of them destined for the hunter's knife. Or it may be the early summer warming of the rivers which lures innumerable spawning salmon to the upper reaches – and to the fishermen's net. Or it may be the shortening evenings of early fall which seem to stir the birds for their southerly migration – or for a short encounter with a stone arrow. In the midst of these easily disturbed processes, Roberts is always alert to the possibility of moments of miraculous balance. One of the minor heroes of his story, Jumping Wolf, takes a journey in early autumn:

> The season of wild harvest was over the land, the days of ripe berries and falling leaves and the flocking birds. Snipe and plover from the farther North, and coveys of ptmarmigan and flocks of snow birds, fed along the ground, and started on quick wings. . . .
> The berry-stained moss on which he reclined was warm as a couch of fox-skins, and the soft bird calls, sounding indolently from hummock and hollow made music in his ears.

Yet the hunter in Roberts' world can easily become the hunted, just as the hero of pantomime must face incalculable perils. Roberts brings this aspect to life at another point in his romance when Jumping Wolf faces almost certain death with four murderous pursuers at his back. Suddenly he sees through the dark wood to the pans of ice on the open lake; he sees "a glimmer of open spaces, a grey glimmer dotted with lighter spots, and in another second he stood at the edge of a great lake whose father shores were hidden in night."

It is against this background of wild naturalistic beauty that the Indians group together in small bands for safety and survival. In small groups of this kind, each individual has a well defined role and usually marked idiosyncrasies as well. Such idiosyncrasies have traditionally been the staple basis of the character types of popular drama and pantomime. Roberts has a sharp eye for the comedy of such quirks, but his characterization transcends the usual stereotype or caricature. One of his most endearing characters is the hero's grandmother, an appealing if hard-handed squaw named Old Blowing Fog. Perhaps she resembles the old grandmother of Micmac tradition or the aged widow of popular drama. But she is no mere stage convention. She has an authenticity which derives from the sharpness with which Roberts focusses the necessities of her life. She is inevitably a tough old lady, having survived the rigours of the remorseless environment for so long. She is a relentless paddler on the long canoe journeys and still carries the heaviest loads on the portage. Her reckless scepticism is as natural as her industry. Her environment seemingly only demands strength and skill. She has little time for any form of magic which does not make itself apparent in terms of size and strength. Confronted by an awesome magician who combines the gentleness of a saint with the authority of a hardened commander, she scornfully remarks "Great magicians were bigger men in my young days." Even after she had disastrously provoked the magician into unleashing a scene of the wild-

est slapstick, she yet has the audacity to belabour a frail but inde-
pendent brave named Old Green Bow (a chauvinist hold-out?) until
his gums rattle. Despite her warlike militancy and her stubborn
refusal to recognize the necessity for a magical counterweight to the
exercise of sheer strength, she easily enough assumes the role of a
ministering angel. She has no hesitation in gently administering a
magic potion (medicine being the preserve of the shaman) to a
desperately sick baby in a mussel shell.

Human life must cling precariously to frail roots in a wild environment such as Roberts' Newfoundland. In view of the power of
the elements in such a setting, it is appropriate that Roberts should
introduce a race of giants into his story. They seem to symbolize the
wild uncontrollable forces of elemental nature – forces for which
Roberts' better protagonists hold a respectful fear and distrust. It is
significant that when the red feathers – a source of a superior form
of power – fall into the hands of these rugged individualists, a scene
of the wildest bedlam is enacted. When the leader of these expo-
nents of the instinct of sheer power, Crack Bone, tries his arm (with
the help of the feathers) at the graceful and farseeing art of flying,
he succeeds only at playing a grotesque form of aeronautical hop-
scotch. The feathers, whose power is strengthened by each generous
act that they further, are intended for those who better understand
the uses of power. The jealousies aroused by Crack Bone's use of
the feathers result in a murky Armageddon, a scene of the wildest
tree smashing (slapstick?) where giant strikes down giant in blind
unreasoning rage. It is hard to say whether it is proper to read a
parable into a scene from a romance of this kind. It may be of
interest to the reader, however, that Theodore Roberts was at one
time a neighbour of the American author Frank Norris, who in
such books as *The Octopus* (1901) exposed the business practices of
the rugged individualists.

What holds one's interest in *The Red Feathers* is the unremitting
nature of the struggle, not a struggle for power or success, but for
the way in which power (as represented by the red feathers) should
be used. Roberts' underlying attitude differs significantly from that
implicit in most of the romances popular in his own day – for the
most part regional or historical novels. The regional novel is typically concerned with the theme of the local boy who makes good; in
terms of Roberts' Newfoundland the cod-fisher who conforms
safely to the accepted mores, corners the market in livers, and mar-
ries a mainland mackerel princess. The historical novel generally
revolves around the elements that culminate in the triumph of one
flag and one national interest. The main interest in both cases tends
to focus on the final outcome and with a rather crudely conceived

notion of success in love, business, or war. Roberts' main focus, by contrast, is not on ends but means. His villain, variously a magician called Bright Robe or a little brown owl is a satirically minded student of the "hopes and vanities" of human nature. He uses his knowledge, particularly his understanding for the thirst for power and possessions, so as to manipulate and dupe his human pawns so that they will serve his ends when they think that they are serving their own. His formidable adversary, Wise-As-A-She-Wolf, on the other hand, is a magician of faith and impulse, one to whom the motivating power of dream is overriding importance. He is a lover of flight, and of vast airy lodges. He does not impose on his friends and allies, but simply helps to focus their impulses. The tension and conflict created by the opposition of these opposed modes of feeling and action are no mere creations of romantic convention to Roberts. The force of the conflict can be felt at every crucial turn in his romance. It is particularly evident in the suppressed power of Roberts' description of titanic invisible battles, ones that faintly shadow the true battle of will involved.

Roberts draws on two strands in the Micmac tradition to develop this main theme of his. The first such strand involves the traditional importance of the Micmac culture hero, Glooscap, a figure comparable with Roberts' Wise-As-A-She-Wolf. One of the most absorbing aspects of the Maritime Algonquin culture is the way in which Glooscap assumes such a central importance in the tradition, one which finds no parallels amongst the Indian traditions of Central Canada. The Ojibwa hero, Wiskejauk, is of altogether minor importance by comparison with Glooscap, the benevolent hero and friend of his tribes. A. G. Bailey, in his article "The Ordeal of the Eastern Algonquins," has pointed out one consequence of Glooscap's central importance when he writes "the belief in mysterious beings, such as the culture hero, provided terms with which the [Maritime Algonquins] could apprehend God." The withdrawal of Glooscap from the mortal sphere would seem to be a natural consequence of such a belief process (although not the only one). It is consistent with Micmac traditions that Roberts' character, Old Blowing Fog, should believe that the great magician is either buried under a mountain, or that he sits "in some gorgeous lodge, beyond the sunset, superior to the affairs of the island in which he has been born." Roberts seems to have a new move in mind for the tradition. His Wise-As-A-She-Wolf takes Old Blowing Fog by surprise, and proves that he is not superior to the island in which he has been born – even to the extent of demolishing the lodges of those that provoke him.

Roberts uses a second strand in the Indian tradition, the legends that surround the shaman with Wendigo tendencies, to develop the character of his evil genius, Bright Robe. Such a figure is a much more typical and central than the culture-hero in most Indian traditions, one who by lonely vigil and through dreams assumes the super-personal powers of an animal manitou or presiding genius and misuses his powers for his own malevolent ends. Like the typical Manitou, Bright Robe in his prime is able to instantaneously transform himself into the shape of animal or bird, and, like the Manitou, he can exercise limited power over man and beast. His appearance as a little brown owl is typical of Indian shaman lore. Yet in his animal shape he preserves a remorseless human venom which his animal counterparts find incomprehensible.

It is the main theme of the book to show how the owl's adversaries try to develop the kind of magical power that can effectively counteract the poison which threatens to infect the entire island. The true nature of the magic is Roberts' secret, one which I leave to the reader to try to discover.

Martin Ware
Dalhousie University

THE
RED FEATHERS

——◆——

CHAPTER I

"RUN - ALL - DAY"

In the days of which I write, in the island now
known as Newfoundland, men made prayers to
the sun, the winds, the frost and the stars. They
believed that giants lived in the north; that a
great stag caribou, as high as a pine, haunted
the wilds beyond the Narrow Sea to the west;
that gods moved about in divers shapes, doing
good or evil as their natures prompted them,
and that certain wise and crafty men acquired a
knowledge of magic and thereby became stronger
than the greatest warriors. Fog, to these people,
was the breath of an old god who lived to the
eastward, just beneath the rim of the sea; and

fire was a spirit, — the offspring of a god, — that sometimes was content to feed on the fagots cut for it, cooking food for men and warming their bodies, and sometimes leaped into the woods and consumed the forest for miles in an outburst of fury.

A man of the Beothic race named Run-all-day had a lodge on the River of Three Fires, about half-way between its mouth and Wind Lake. There he lived only in the warmer months of the year. At the approach of winter he followed the great herds of caribou farther inland and southward, to the deeper forest and more sheltered barrens. During the summer he netted and speared the salmon in the River of Three Fires, feeding himself and his family on the flesh and smoking what could not be used then for their winter supply. Early in October, before starting on the inland journey, his wife and children gathered nuts and berries, while he hunted the fat caribou, which were already gathering in great herds preparatory to moving to the more sheltered feeding-grounds. With the venison and the berries his wife, Red Willow, made a rough sort of pemmican.

Run-all-day was fleet of foot and strong of

wind and leg. It was by his speed and endurance when a boy that he had won his name. He had also proved himself a warrior of prowess, when occasion demanded, and might have followed his father as chief of a clan; but the islanders happened to be entering on a long term of peace when he grew to manhood, so he took a wife from another village and journeyed away from his family. His wits were not as quick as his legs and he entertained no great ambitions of distinguishing himself. He was quite content to protect and provide for his family — to sleep warm and eat his fill all the year round and see them do the same. Of course, sometimes at the tail-end of a bad season, provisions ran low; but if any man could find game and bring it to the ground, it was Run-all-day.

On a certain June evening, when the west was red and dusk was settling along the edges of the woods, Run-all-day withdrew his net of raw-hide thongs from a big pool four miles above his wigwam and seated himself on the grassy bank for a few minutes' rest before walking home. Nine great silver fish lay beside him — a respectable load even for Run-all-day. To lessen their weight he had already slit them from throat to tail, with his flint knife, and tossed the entrails into the bushes. He was well satisfied with his afternoon's work, and sighed with contentment and a pleasant weariness.

" It has been a good summer," he murmured, " and there will be plenty of food for all of us." He smiled at that thought, for his family had increased by one within the past week.

" You are a fortunate man, Run-all-day," said a voice at his shoulder.

In the fraction of a second the salmon fisher was turned and on his feet, with the flint blade with which he had cleaned the fish ready in his hand. His eyes encountered those of a young man who stood not ten feet distant, with his back to the dusky forest. The stranger's tunic of dressed deer-skin was decorated with strings of polished stones. On his feet were finely worked moccasins and in his hand a short spear. His face was very kind. To a keener reader of mankind than Run-all-day it would have suggested the hope and faith of a child, the wisdom that comes of experience and the charitable spirit of old age.

" Though I may be a stranger to you," said the young man, smiling, " I am not your enemy.

You need not threaten me with the knife, oh, tireless runner."

Run-all-day tossed his weapon beside the dead fish and looked steadily at the other.

" You do not belong to this river, chief," said he, " and yet you call me by my name. Is my reputation so great in the world? "

" To those who have ears to hear of an honest man," replied the stranger, " your reputation has travelled far. How is the little warrior that came to your lodge but five days ago? "

" He is well and sound," answered Run-all-day. " But what do you know of him? " he asked, in wonder. " Are you a god? "

" You put the question honestly," said the young man with the spear.

He stepped close to the salmon fisher.

" I am not a god," he said. " I am even of your own clan. I am called Wise-as-a-she-wolf."

Run-all-day looked at him in open astonishment, for the name of the great magician was known far and wide. Some people held that Wise-as-a-she-wolf was stronger than several of the gods themselves; that he was the greatest student of magic since the days of the wicked Bright Robe; that his magic had been learned in the Crimson Wigwam and in the White Lodge beyond the ramparts of eternal ice; that the secrets of immortality and everlasting youth were his. And yet 'twas said that for all his power, his heart was kind as a young girl's.

" Great chief," said the salmon fisher, at last, " I had thought to see, in Wise-as-a-she-wolf, a full-grown man."

" So be it, friend," replied the other, and, in the twinkling of an eye, a warrior of great stature and grim visage stood before Run-all-day.

" Have mercy, great chief," cried the fisherman of the River of Three Fires. He was strong and courageous; but he had a dread of big magic.

" Have no fear of your kinsman," laughed the other; and, in the next second, the youth with the gentle face laid a reassuring hand on Run-all-day's shoulder. The gigantic warrior was gone.

CHAPTER II

THE TWO RED FEATHERS

"I AM hungry and weary," said Wise-as-a-she-wolf.

"My cooking-pot is full," replied the other, "and I have many soft skins for bedding; but I fear me, chief, that to sleep in my lodge you will first have to practise magic on the throat of the new warrior, or on your own ears."

"Nay, friend, a couch in the open will suit my taste," replied the youth. "So that the young warrior is not in pain, let him yell. 'Tis the great spirit of him giving voice against the littleness of his body and the weakness of his legs."

So they set out for the fisherman's wigwam, each carrying a load of the silver fish. The cooking fire was burning brightly when they stepped from the woods, and the slender form of Singing Bird, eldest child of Run-all-day and Red Willow, was seen bending above the tree stump, that had been hollowed to serve as a pot,

which stood near the fire. The stew in the pot
was boiling vigorously, for the girl had dropped
stones into it which she had first heated near to
the bursting-point among the coals of the fire.
Two smaller figures — and these of boys —
skipped about in the ruddy glow and shouted
that they were quite ready for their meal; still
another was seen dabbling in the shallow water
at the edge of the river; and from the interior
of the pointed lodge sounded the crying of an
infant.

Wise-as-a-she-wolf let his string of fish slip to
the grass, and looked at the scene before him with
something of amusement and something of
consternation in his face.

" A fine family," he remarked. " And surely
that littlest warrior has the voice of a great chief."

Run-all-day was highly delighted at these
words, being as foolish in such matters as are
the fathers of our own time. With a self-satisfied
grunt, he led the stranger to a seat by the fire
and fetched him a bark cup full of spring water,
that he might quench his thirst before eating.

The magician ate very little for a hungry
youth, and yet the stew was excellent. Before
he touched the food, he was seen to cast aside

from his waist a girdle of white leather painted
with many wonderful figures of gods and men
and beasts. He slept well that night, on a couch
of bear skins, in the shelter of a spruce which
stood midway between the lodge and the fire.
He was awakened, in the early morning, by the
voice of Singing Bird. Opening his eyes, he beheld her busy at the cooking-fire, singing as she
worked.

The breakfast was as good as the evening meal;
and the magician, pointing to the belt which hung
loosely above his hips, said, " You are fortunate,
my friend. You have no need, with such a cook,
of a magic Hunger Belt like this." His gaze
rested kindly on Singing Bird.

" But the meat must first be caught, chief,"
replied Run-all-day.

When Wise-as-a-she-wolf was ready to continue
his journey, the fisherman walked from the camp
with him, for a short distance.

" I am going northward," said the magician,
" on very urgent business. I have had dealings
with many great people — even with the gods —
and so I have awakened envy in more than one
dark heart. For all my magic, friend, my life
is not so good a one as yours. You love and are

loved. You keep your family fed and are at peace with the world. No evil magic is worked against you and the wrath of the gods is aimed so high that it goes over your head. I have my days of glory and my victories; but strange weapons are ever being shaped for my undoing."

"Yes, chief, I am content with my humble life," replied Run-all-day.

The young man placed two small red feathers in the other's hand.

"These are for the littlest warrior," he said. "They are great magic — great for good or evil, as the heart prompts. When he is large enough to run here and there, place one of these feathers in each of his moccasins, flat on the sole of his foot. Let him cherish them, for they will help him in his play, and, later, in the chase, and they have the power to save him even from death."

At the last word he stepped aside from the trail and was gone, with no more noise than the slipping away of a shadow.

Run-all-day continued to stare at the spot where Wise-as-a-she-wolf had so lately stood, for fully a minute. This magic was no light thing. Courageous though he was, his legs shook under him as if with cold. A dozen sea-eagles could not have made him flinch; but he trembled at the touch of the two little feathers in his hand.

" He is a great man," he said at last, " and possessed of wonderful magic; but perhaps he was not wise in his gift to the littlest warrior. Magic is for gods and mighty chieftains; it is too potent a thing for humble folks like me and mine. Did he not say himself, but a moment ago, that power breeds powerful enemies and that even the gods bend their ears to the affairs of magicians? "

He gazed fearfully at the bright feathers in his hand.

" He is a great chief; a kind and a good young man, a cousin of the gods, I do not doubt, — but I fear he has made a mistake. He has been too generous."

He let the feathers fall from his hand to the moss at the side of the trail, turned quickly and hastened back to the clearing and the lodge.

He found Red Willow lying on a couch of soft skins, well and happy. Old Blowing Fog, her mother, squatted beside her with the baby in her wrinkled arms.

" The stranger has gone," said Run-all-day.

" He is a great magician and his name is Wise-as-a-she-wolf.   But he envied me my humble contentment, for all of that.   He gave me two red feathers, for a gift for that little warrior, and said that they are possessed of magic power; and then he was gone, like the first whiff of smoke from a newly lighted fire."

" Where are the feathers? " inquired Red Willow, her face aglow with interest.

The brave shook his head and smiled wisely.

" The gift was meant well," he said; " but a man must judge of some things for himself, even if he be but a hunter and fisherman. Magic may be well enough for the great men whose feet are set in high places; though I think even they would be safer without it. They may hunt with the gods and the north lights if they please; but the meat of the caribou and beaver is better suited to my taste."

" And what does all this grand talk lead to? " asked old Blowing Fog.

" I dropped the feathers on the ground and let them lie," said the man.

" Then what do I see in your belt? " asked the old woman, peering between half-closed lids.

Run-all-day put his hand to his leather girdle —

and drew out the two red feathers. He gasped. His swarthy cheeks turned white as the bark of the birch. Had one of those little, fat savages from the frozen west (who sometimes crossed the Narrow Sea and fought with the islanders) appeared and stuck a spear into his flesh, he could not have looked more horrified.

"Give them to me. I do not fear their magic," cried Red Willow.

Run-all-day obeyed her with a sigh of relief. He would face the magician himself — but those little, slim, red feathers — ah, they made his blood run cold as ice. Red Willow took them fearlessly and admired their bright colour; and yet she was in the habit of fleeing, with covered head, from bats flickering in the twilight. She laughed at her big, trembling husband.

"It is foolish to throw away a gift," she said. "And it is even more foolish to run away from two little feathers that were given you by a friend."

Old Blowing Fog laughed, as she rocked the baby in her arms.

"When I was young we saw greater magic than that, almost every day," said she. "My father once worked such magic on his bow that it shot the arrows so high into the air that they never came down."

"But I've heard that he couldn't shoot a standing caribou, for all that," replied the man, recovering something of his assurance. He often argued with Blowing Fog.

"Give me honest arrows, honest muscles and honest feathers sticking in the tails of honest birds," he continued. "I do not need any magic, old or new, to keep the pot full of meat and fish and the rain out of my lodge. And I'd feel like a fool shooting my arrows so high in the air that they'd never come down."

Both the women laughed at him.

"Oh, I am wiser than you think," said he, and stalked out of the lodge. But he left the two magic feathers in Red Willow's hand.

CHAPTER III

THE LITTLEST WARRIOR AND HIS SUMMER HOME

THE home in which the baby had been born was only a hut, built of poles and sheets of bark. It was a fine house, though, for the time and country. Its door was the hide of a caribou, — and how fearfully that great hide flapped and bulged inward at the pressure of the night winds. Fortunately the season was June, when the air was warm and the sun shone almost every day.

When the littlest warrior was a few weeks old, he was put into a bag of furry skins fastened to a light framework of wood. In this he rested all day, in an upright position, sometimes against one of the poles of the lodge, and sometimes on the back of his mother, or Blowing Fog, or little Singing Bird.

He was a good baby, crying only when he was very hungry or when he was bathed in the cold water of the river. He spent the greater part of his time in sleep. Even when awake he did not seem to take much interest in what went on around him; but this indifference to the world was apparent in him only in his earliest days. At the age of two months he began to show signs (so said his mother and Blowing Fog) of an exceptional spirit and intellect; but, to the casual observer, it would have seemed that he but howled with a more powerful voice and kicked and struggled with lustier limbs.

It was only during the summer months — from May to October — that Run-all-day and his family lived in the little clearing beside the River of Three Fires. There was no other wigwam within ten miles of them; for at this time the small tribes, or clans, of the north and south, the east and west, were at peace with one another and so the people did not have to band together, in villages, in self-defence. Sometimes, during the summer, people of their own tribe passed up or down the stream in front of their lodge, in skin-covered canoes of unwieldy shapes.

Many of Run-all-day's friends spent the summer months on the coast of the great sea-bays, where they caught cod-fish to cure for winter use. Some lived close to the great salt water all the year round, and slaughtered a few of the hosts of seals that floated down from the north, on the grinding ice floes, early in the spring. Others, like Run-all-day, pitched their summer lodges on the rivers and ponds, moving southward and further inland, with the great herds of caribou, at the approach of winter.

The hunting of the caribou began early in September, when the calves of that year had grown strong enough to live independently of their mothers. Several of the families returning from the bays, halted for awhile in their journey and joined Run-all-day in the chase. Now the youngest baby heard more noise than usual. Strange faces bent above him and strange arms lifted him to feel his weight. Several cooking-fires burned before the lodge; canoes of many models were drawn up on the bank; everybody seemed to be happy and busy. But soon the caribou began to travel southward, across the great barrens and through the low, dark timber. Then dried fish and meat, skins and weapons were made into packs, and canoes were launched and headed up stream.

Now the littlest warrior opened his eyes with more concern for the everyday affairs of life. He cried less than ever before in his brief career and smiled more readily. Even when he was placed in a canoe, still in his fur bag, beside his mother, he did not make any violent signs of objection. His father and all the family effects were at his back. Close in front sat his three small brothers, and Singing Bird, and in the bow old Blowing Fog plied a broad paddle.

Fortunately for all concerned, the canoe was both large and strong and steady — a masterpiece among canoes. Run-all-day had built it during the previous winter. He had planned a model for the frame to suit the size of his family and had constructed it of light, well-seasoned spruce. Being short of hides at the time, he had covered the frame with great sheets of tough, white bark from the birch trees of the forest. This bark was much lighter than caribou hides, and he had felt angry with himself for never having thought to use it before in boat building. For years, he had known that it was proof against water, for had it not sheltered him ever since his birth, from rain and sleet? He had stitched the seams with root-fibres and daubed them thoroughly with a mixture of gum and fat.

Run-all-day's friends had laughed at the new canoe and its builder, and had advised the brave not to venture on the river in so novel a craft. The whole world, they said, covered its canoes with skin; then why should he do otherwise? But Run-all-day had hardened his heart against their warnings and jeers and gone his own way; and it had proved to be a right way.

Now a little fleet of six canoes toiled steadily up the river. Though Run-all-day's craft was larger and more heavily loaded than any, it soon outdistanced them all. The brave, standing upright in the stern, used a long pole and Blowing Fog dug vigorously at the water with her broad paddle. Sometimes swift rapids churned and snarled in front of them, defying them to ascend. Then all the bundles of fish and meat and skins, the weapons and the children, had to be unloaded. Then the canoe was lifted from the stream and carried along the shore, to the top of the swift water, by Run-all-day and Blowing Fog. Everyone but the baby helped to portage the cargo.

Shortly after sunset, Run-all-day's canoe was run ashore at the edge of a little meadow, again unloaded and lifted out of the water. Soon a fire was lighted and the comforting fragrance of broiling venison stole wide on the air. Dusk had fallen by the time the other voyagers reached the camp.

CHAPTER IV

BRIGHT ROBE TELLS A STORY OF THE RED FEATHERS

THE men of the party sat late around the fire, telling stories of prowess at the fishing and in the chase. Some of them even talked of the battle-field, for they were all of one clan. They had been at war with the people of the south and south-west, not many years before. Run-all-day was no more backward in story-telling than in other matters. He was a skilled and tireless hunter, and he did not object to the fact becoming known to the general public. Simply, he praised his birch-bark canoe; his speed and endurance in running down a wounded deer; his summer's work at the fishing; even his wife and his family were bragged about — and surely no one had ever before possessed such an admirable mother-in-law. Some of the braves grunted at that, for they knew that Run-all-day and old Blowing Fog often disagreed on household matters.

Suddenly one of the cod-fishers, who was called

Lazy Bear, threw a large piece of drift-wood into the heart of the fire. Sparks and flames shot upward, and, for a few seconds, the whole camp was lit by the redoubled radiance.

And there, at one end of the semi-circle of braves, sat a stranger with a robe of bright fur on his back. A gasp of astonishment arose from the fishers and hunters. Lazy Bear almost stepped into the fire, in the first flash of amazement. A dozen hands went to the hafts of clubs and flint knives.

" Good evening to you, chief," said Run-all-day, in a voice that was not altogether steady.

But the stranger made no reply, and the man nearest him edged away to the left.

" Have you no tongue?" cried Run-all-day, with anger in his voice. Anger always ate up fear, in the breast of the salmon fisher.

The stranger raised his head and stared at the speaker with dark and glowing eyes. But he did not open his lips. His piercing, insolent gaze would have daunted a weaker man than Run-all-day; but it only stirred the great hunter's anger to higher flame, even as the drift-wood had worked upon the smouldering heart of the fire.

" If you have no tongue," said Run-all-day,

" make us a sign. You have come, unbidden, to our camp. The haft of my club itches in my hand."

" Brave words," said the stranger, in a voice cold as a wind off the ice floe. " Lift your club, — if you can."

Run-all-day's weapon lay beside him on the moss of the little clearing. His right hand closed on the stick and he made a slight effort to swing the stone head upward, over his shoulder. He turned and applied both hands and all his strength to the task. But the stone head of the weapon that was usually like a toy in his hands, would not leave the ground. A sweat of fear burst out on him and he loosed the haft of the club as if it were red hot. A thrill of apprehension went through the semi-circle of braves, at sight of their comrade's half-seen actions.

The stranger laughed without mirth.

" Great hunter, great slayer and smoker of salmon, when next Bright Robe comes to your camp and honours you by taking a seat at your fire, refrain from clamouring for explanations," he said.

The name of Bright Robe drove the last sparks of courage and anger from the breasts of Run-all-day's companions. Run-all-day, however, felt the sullen rage still alive under the outward chill of fear.

"You have heard of me," continued the unwelcome guest, "and of this robe, which is made of the pelt of one wolf — of one of the great, white wolves that hunt under the north lights, in the land of eternal ice."

True, they had all heard of Bright Robe, the master of magicians. Their mothers had frightened them, when they were children, with tales of his fearful and wonderful doings; and they, in their turn, had heard the stories from their mothers and grandmothers. Legend recorded that, in a fit of anger, he had once defied a god; and many were the versions of the tale of his punishment. But he had vanished from the island, and that was the great thing, for he had been the most wicked as well as the most powerful of all the magicians that had practised their arts since the beginning of the world. And now, after a hundred summers of banishment, here he sat by the fire of honest hunters and fishermen, with the silver robe gleaming on his shoulders. Was he stronger than the gods themselves?

Even the courage of Run-all-day melted again.

What had brought this awful visitor to their humble fire?

Several members of the party hastened to bring food and water to the great magician, who ate ravenously.

"I have made a weary journey," said he, at last. "I have spent eight days in travelling a distance that, had I not been robbed, I should have accomplished in a few hours. I, who owned the red feathers but a moon ago, bruised my feet on rocks and roots like any common fellow."

Run-all-day stood beyond the smoke of the fire and so Bright Robe did not notice the sudden alertness of the hunter's face and body.

"What are these red feathers, mighty chief?" inquired Lazy Bear, who possessed curiosity to the extent that he lacked energy.

Food had mollified the magician's spirit. "The red feathers," said he, "are articles of great magic. The man who wears them against his feet can outrace the flying hawk, and only he who wears the moccasins of the wind can overtake him in the air."

"I have heard old people talk of the magic moccasins that carry a man with the speed of a flying teal, but I have heard no stories of the red feathers," said Run-all-day.

He spoke in a voice that showed no more than a polite interest in the subject.

" Many stories are told of the moccasins," said Bright Robe, " for they have changed hands many times, but have never left this country, in hundreds of years, for more than two moons. The red feathers, however, are not known to the old story-tellers. Maybe they have thought that all the swift running was done by the moccasins of the wind. It was in the time of the coldest winter, when the Narrow Sea was bound with ice from shore to shore, that the red feathers came into the possession of a chief of this country. Mountaineers from the hills under the setting sun crossed the Narrow Sea — and with them came many of those fierce little men of the north — and did battle with the nations of this island. The leader of the invaders sped here and there in the air, swift as a chasing hawk, swooping and slaying like a hawk among grouse. To every man he killed, terror was burned into the hearts of a score. Our warriors had no strength to bend their bows against him, or hurl their war-clubs, when they heard the whisper of his flying feet.

But one man kept his courage alive and his eyes ready. His was a strong bow, and his arrows were long and sharply barbed. Slipping from the central tumult of the battle, he crouched beneath a spruce tree and peered about for the flying enemy as a hunter looks out of cover for homing geese. Suddenly he saw the terrible one flash down upon the struggling warriors; saw him strike once, and twice, and leap into the air again. With lessened speed he drew near the spruce tree under which the Beothic chief crouched ready. The bow bent and sprang straight, and, with a fearful cry, the man of the flying feet struggled in the air. Another arrow whined and struck — and another found its mark — and then the terrible invader fell, like a stone, to the earth. And, in the moccasins of the warrior from across the Narrow Sea, the chief who slew him found the red feathers."

The men around the fire had followed the story with breathless interest. For the time being, their fear of the narrator was forgotten.

"The coldest winter was many hundreds of seasons ago," said one, "and never since then has our country been in such danger. It must have been a mighty battle."

"It was a mighty battle," replied Bright Robe. "I was young then — I am older than I look — and had learned nothing of magic. I fought in the battle, for I was born in the tribe that dwells on the coast of the Narrow Sea."

"Was it you, great chief, who slew the leader of the enemy?" asked Run-all-day.

"Nay," replied the magician, with a low chuckle. "But two days after the invaders were driven away from our shores, out onto the ice that was already weakening and breaking, I took the red feathers from the moccasin of that great chief and put them in my own."

"Then he must have been sleeping," said Run-all-day.

"A sound sleep, in truth," replied Bright Robe, calmly.

"You killed him — a chief of your own tribe — for the magic feathers," cried the hunter.

"Verily, oh smoker of fish and flesh," replied the magician. "And many another have I killed, for less than those red feathers. To regain possession of them now I should consider the speeding of an hundred lives a niggardly payment."

" We know nothing of the feathers," cried an old man.

Others confirmed the statement, in broken words and tremulous gestures.

Bright Robe sneered. " You may save your breath," said he. " No cleaner of cod stole the prize from the feet of Bright Robe; of that, I need no assurance. Only the gods, and Wise-as-a-she-wolf, have the hardihood to strike at me. Even now I am on the trail of my enemy. It will be a long trail, for he has both the moccasins of the wind and the red feathers — but when one knows the secret of everlasting life one can afford to travel slowly."

He looked about him with his dark, glowing eyes. The braves at the fire felt their muscles loosen under the awful glance.

" Now bring me thirty days' food, dried meat and smoked fish enough to last a man thirty days," he ordered. " I do not intend to delay my journey for the purpose of killing caribou," he added.

Run-all-day and his companions were glad enough that the magician asked for so little. They hastened to bring the best of their meat and fish and pemmican. They heaped it near their unwelcome visitor, in the light of the fire.

"Now bind it securely into one pack," he ordered.

When this was done he arose from the ground and, bending over the great pack, laid his hand on it. In a moment it had dwindled to the size of a crouching wolf — to the size of a man's head — to the smallness of a hazel nut. And this tiny object he picked up, between finger and thumb, and tucked somewhere under his belt.

"You are worthy people," he said, looking around, well pleased at the wonder, fear, and admiration written on the faces of the hunters.

"Now I continue my journey," he added. "See, I draw my robe of white fur over my head so that not a man of you shall be able to say which way I went."

At the last word he drew the robe above his shoulders — and lo, the fearful magician was nowhere to be seen.

For hours the hunters continued to sit by the fire. They were afraid that Bright Robe might still be lurking near them, to hear what they had to say of him. So they praised him warmly to each other, until they could not keep their eyelids open another minute.

CHAPTER V

RUN-ALL-DAY'S NEW-FOUND AMBITION

WIND LAKE was entered early in the evening of the second day of the journey. The voyagers did not land at sunset, but continued to paddle up the long, narrow lake until they reached a point on the western shore where a wooded valley opened on the water, between two wooded hills. By the time all the canoes were unloaded and the people settled for sleep, it was long past midnight.

This was the place where Run-all-day had spent the last four winters, his lodge standing alone in that warm and sheltered valley, with an outlook on the white lake, and with good hunting country on three sides; but now the owners of the other canoes and families begged him to allow them to build their winter lodges beside his.

"Let us stay near you," said an old man named Green Bow on the morning after their arrival. "The visit of Bright Robe has filled us with trembling, and our dreams with black visions. You are brave. You shall be chief of the village and master of the chase, if only we may camp in your valley and keep our hearts up with the sight of your courage; for who can say at what time Bright Robe may visit us again? "

" My heart ran to water in the presence of Bright Robe," replied Run-all-day. " My muscles were no more than the muscles of a woman. I did his bidding like a child and trembled at the sound of his voice. And yet," he concluded, wonderingly, " you ask me to inspire you with my courage."

" Your eyes remained steady," replied the old man. " I think there was still a flame of courage in the bottom of your heart."

Run-all-day looked from the old man to the others of the party, and a new and delightful sensation took possession of him. Here was recognition of his prowess, surely. They looked to him for protection from the great and wicked magician. Well, he would do what he could, as he had always done in humbler matters.

" Friends," said he, " I am willing to be your chief and to let you hunt and live in this valley. But I am not a magician, and I greatly fear that the courage of a hunter would prove of no avail against the evil strength of Bright Robe. But, my friends, I am well liked by one who does not fear Bright Robe. Wise-as-a-she-wolf has claimed me for a relative; has partaken of my cooking-pot; has even made a gift to my littlest warrior."

Now this was a trifle more than even Lazy Bear could believe. As for old Green Bow, he frowned at Run-all-day. "This is a new thing to our ears," he said. "May I ask, chief, how long it is since you began to keep such fine company?"

The new-made chief was stung to anger.

"You do not believe my word," he cried. "Then I will give you proof of it."

He put his hand on Green Bow's shoulder. "Where did you have your lodge, during the summer?" he asked, sternly.

"At the mouth of the River of Three Fires, on a knoll on the northern shore, under three great pines," answered the old man.

"And did you leave any familiar possession behind you?"

The old man nodded.

"I forgot my best skinning-knife," he replied. "It is somewhere in my wigwam, chief."

" Then," said Run-all-day, gazing proudly around him at the puzzled faces of his people, " I shall start for the mouth of the river to-night, — and in the morning the knife will be in your hand."

" Ah-ha," cried Green Bow. " Then you are a magician after all. Why did you not lift your club, two nights ago, and deal Bright Robe a whack on the head? "

" So you continue to doubt me," said Run-all-day. " But I do not wonder at that. I am an honest fisherman and hunter. I have no knowledge of magic. But if I fail to bring you your knife by sunrise to-morrow, then you may choose another chief and Run-all-day will take his family from this valley and seek another home."

The braves were still incredulous. Though of great endurance and speed, how could their comrade make a four days' journey in one night?

" Perhaps you have the moccasins of the wind hidden in your lodge? " said Lazy Bear.

" Or the red feathers? " suggested a youth named Little Fox.

Green Bow placed his fingers on his lips. " Would you have Bright Robe back again? " he whispered, sharply. " Keep your thoughts behind your tongues, if your minds run on such things."

"The old man is right," said Run-all-day. "If I make a long journey in the night-time, to prove to you that I still speak the truth, let not so much as a hint of it go beyond the warriors of this new village."

Run-all-day worked busily with the others, at the building of the lodges. But the furtive glances and whisperings of his companions kept him in a bad humour; and thought of the awful journey he had so boastfully undertaken, weighed on his spirit. He did not doubt, for a moment, the ability of the red feathers to take him to the mouth of the river and home again; but fear of the terrific speed and the great magic gripped his heart.

When the evening meal was finished and the warriors began to draw around the central fire, the new chief entered his lodge and whispered his trouble in the ear of Red Willow.

"You may not withdraw from your promise," she said. "If these are truly the magic feathers they will not fail you. Fly high and straight, tarry at Green Bow's camp only long enough to find the knife, and return without again alighting.

It is well that you planned to make the journey in the night-time; for, doubt not, sharp eyes would mark your flight by day, eager tongues would carry word of it far and wide, and the ears of powerful persons would hear of it. Now, since the visit of Bright Robe, I, too, fear this gift for the littlest warrior. But it is our duty to keep the feathers safely. Wise-as-a-she-wolf may need them again. We must never allow them to pass into the hands of one of his enemies."

Run-all-day placed one of the slim, red feathers in each of his moccasins, with shaking fingers. Then, for several hours, he sat in the lodge, listening to the chatter of his family, and struggling with the fear that ran like ice in his veins. At last he stepped softly through the doorway, followed by Red Willow. The night was black, unlit by any star, and a low wind crawled in the tree-tops.

The woman pointed northward. "That is the road," she whispered.

Run-all-day drew a deep breath, hesitated for a moment, and then sprang into the air. He saw the dark mass of the forest under his feet, and the glow of the camp-fire around which the warriors still sat. The four quarters of the sky lay black and vast around him, and the prowling wind blew

against his moccasins. Then, with a second
desperate resolve, he ran northward along the
currents of the air.

Dawn was breaking along the east when Run-
all-day entered his lodge with Green Bow's knife
in his hand. He was breathless. Snow had commenced to fall when he had but begun his return
journey, and he had lost his way and been forced
to descend twice to earth. He returned the
feathers to Red Willow with a sigh of relief.

When the sun crawled up in a clear sky, he
stepped from the lodge and approached the group
of braves already assembled in the centre of the
encampment. The experience of the night had
left a pallor on his face; and every man noticed
it.

" You have not slept well," said old Green Bow,
peering up at him with a secret glance.

" Have you worried about your good hunting-
ground? " inquired Little Fox.

For answer, Run-all-day took the knife from
his belt and tossed it to Green Bow.

" Is that your wonderful skinning-knife? " he
asked, sharply.

The old man recovered the weapon from the
ground, examined it closely and uttered a hoarse

cry of amazement. The others crowded around him; only the chief held aloof.

"It is the knife," cried one.

"He left it at the mouth of the river, four days' journey from here," cried another.

"I keep my promises," said Run-all-day, and stalked back to his lodge.

CHAPTER VI

RUN-ALL-DAY VISITS WHISPERING GRASS

THE first winter of Run-all-day's chieftainship passed quietly in the wooded valley on Wind Lake. No magicians came to the little village, and the magic feathers remained safe in Red Willow's care. Between the night of the chief's great journey and the freezing of the lake, many caribou were killed. Later, bear, and wolf, fox, marten, and wild-cat fell to the spoil of the hunters. The women and larger children, and the old men, worked at dressing the skins for robes and clothing, at making arrows and bows and snow-shoes.

Run-all-day's youngest child grew steadily, in the shelter of the big lodge. In fine weather, Singing Bird often carried him about the clearing and even out on the frozen lake. Old Blowing Fog made him a coat of fox-skins to wear out-of-doors.

When spring came, and the snow melted on the barrens and dwindled in the woods, and swollen waters and soft winds gnawed the floor of ice that hid the lake, the baby in the chief's lodge began to fret and lose weight. Red Willow and Blowing Fog were good nurses and knew something of the use of medicinal herbs; but, day by day, the little warrior weakened.

Run-all-day hung about the lodge, anxious and helpless. On the morning of the third day of the baby's illness old Green Bow caught him by the sleeve.

"Whispering Grass is a good doctor," he said. "She lives on the Highest Hill, beyond this lake and Great Devil's Lake, westward and southward. For a warm cloak of marten skins she would give you medicine to cure the little warrior. Three winters ago, when I was hunting in those lands, she saved me from a fever that was eating my blood."

"Three winters ago," exclaimed the chief. "How do you know that she is still there?"

"She will live nowhere else."

"But she may be dead."

"You will know, when you arrive at her lodge."

"But it is a long journey, and the baby is very ill," cried Run-all-day.

"You made a longer journey to bring me my knife," replied Green Bow.

Run-all-day turned from him and entered the lodge. Hope and resolve shone in his eyes.

"Give me the feathers," he whispered to Red Willow. "I must make a long journey, for medicine for the littlest warrior; and I may not wait for the darkness to conceal my flight."

In a few seconds the red feathers were inside his moccasins, against the soles of his feet. He bent above the sick child, where it lay in the arms of Blowing Fog, and touched the colourless lips with his fingers.

"Keep a brave heart, little warrior. The gift of the good magician will fight for you," he said.

He was about to step from the lodge when Red Willow detained him with a gesture of the hand.

"Should Bright Robe, or any friend of his, see you, he must not know who it is that runs on the wind," she said, quietly lifting a long garment of mink skins, almost black in colour, to his shoulders.

"Belt it about you," she said, "and draw the hood close around your face."

Run-all-day obeyed her swiftly, then stepped from the lodge to the outer brightness.

"I go now in search of Whispering Grass," he said to Green Bow, who stood without.

"May good fortune attend you," replied the old man, staring with an expression of awe at the chief's feet.

Without more ado, Run-all-day faced west and south and sprang into the air. Now the gleaming, sunlit wilderness lay soft and familiar under his wide vision, and there was no fear in his heart save for the sick child. With all his strength, he set his feet to the air and sped away on his journey. The mottled expanse of Wind Lake was passed in a few seconds. Rushing above the barrens beyond, he overtook and passed a flying crow. He saw a wooded hollow, a few lodges in a little clearing, and a boy gazing up at him, with astonished eyes, and it was as if he had but looked down, for a moment, at a painted picture. He passed over hills, his speeding feet almost brushing the crowded tree-tops. He saw caribou, in vast herds, feeding and moving. They seemed no more than toys made by an old woman.

Soon, Run-all-day saw Great Devil's Lake in front of him. It was long and narrow, and split for more than half its length by a slim, wooded island. In some places the water already shone in dark pools among the rotting ice. Beyond, stood a range of hills, from which one cone rose

higher than any mountain-top in sight. He did
not doubt that this was the hill of the medicine
woman; but his heart shook at the thought that
he might find there only a deserted lodge. As
he approached the hill he ascended into higher and
rarer altitudes of air, eager to read the fate of his
journey in one sweeping glance.

Pausing in his flight, so high above the wilderness that the forests looked like moss, he beheld
a tiny wigwam half-way up the southern slope
of the hill, with a feather of smoke at its roof.
Then, in great circles ever descending, he swooped
to the little clearing. Throwing aside his robe of
mink skins, he hastened to the door of the lodge
and peered within. He could only see the glow
of a little fire, for his eyes had narrowed against
the vasts of sunlight.

"Enter, chief," said an aged voice.

But Run-all-day stepped back a pace, still
with his eyes on the black interior of the lodge.

"I seek Whispering Grass, the great doctor,"
he said.

"I am Whispering Grass," replied the voice.
"Enter, chief, and tell your errand."

By this time Run-all-day could make out the
form of the old woman, crouched above a pot

near the fire. Assuring himself that no other
human being lurked in the shadows of the lodge
he obeyed her summons. A strange, bitter-sweet
odour filled the wigwam, and all around, from the
sloping sides of bark, hung wisps of herbs and
leaves.

Run-all-day told his name to the old woman,
and that he had heard of her from Green Bow.
Then he asked for medicine for his baby, and
described the infant's sickness as best he could.

"And what will you pay, chief?" she asked.

The question reminded him that he had forgotten to bring a gift of furs, as Green Bow had
suggested; but he bethought himself of the great
robe of mink skins which he had worn in the
flight.

"Get the medicine ready," he said, "and I will
fetch the gift. I left it at the edge of the clearing."

"And what is it?" she asked, fixing her bright
eyes on his face.

"It is a great robe, made of fifty mink skins,"
he replied.

"Good," she cried. "Bring it quickly, so that
the virtue of my gratitude may enter into the
medicine."

Run-all-day crossed the clearing in one step,

having forgotten the feathers in his moccasins. He returned more cautiously, with the robe in his arms.

Whispering Grass was delighted with the gift. She spread it wide on the ground and felt every inch of the fur with her wrinkled hands, crooning all the while.

" I am in a hurry," the chief reminded her. " The child is near death."

At that the old woman set to work. She placed a small vessel of clay near the fire, filled it with the liquor from the pot and added a few crimson berries, some thread-like golden roots and a pinch of white powder. She stirred the mixture with a stick. Her movements were very deliberate.

" Hurry! Hurry! " exclaimed Run-all-day.

Whispering Grass did not so much as turn her head.

" You should have the medicines already prepared," cried the brave.

At that, the old woman snorted defiantly, but continued stirring the brew as slowly as ever. At last she set the vessel away from the fire.

" Nobody but old Whispering Grass can make such fine medicine as that," she mumbled. " It is worth a hundred robes of mink skins."

"If it cures the little warrior of his illness, then shall I give you a hundred more robes like this," said Run-all-day.

"Nay, chief," she replied. "One will more than outlast my remaining season of life. It is a rich gift. I have steeped my precious herbs, before now, for no more than a few dried fish."

"Is the medicine ready?" inquired the chief.

"Yes, but how will you carry it on so long a journey?" asked the woman.

"As it is," he replied, lifting the vessel of clay from the ground and striding from the lodge. A hundred yards or so from the clearing, he placed the precious medicine on a rock from which the snow had melted. Then he tore a quantity of small, well-feathered branches from the spruce trees within reach and fastened them about his body, for a disguise. He bound them tightly with his leather belt. The branches hung along his legs and stood above his shoulders.

"Should any one see me on the homeward flight," he said, "he will think I am the father of all the eagles."

None of the precious liquor was spilled on the trip from the Highest Hill to Wind Lake; in fact, it was scarcely yet cool when Run-all-day stepped into his lodge.

" Here is the great medicine," he said, and gave the clay vessel into Blowing Fog's hands. Red Willow was holding the baby, who was lying very still in her arms. The old woman seemed to know the medicine for, after tasting it, she grunted with satisfaction. She dipped out some of the liquid in a mussel shell and poured it between the infant's colourless lips.

" My mother often made this same medicine," she mumbled. " Had I but the proper roots and herbs, I could brew it myself."

It pleased her, poor old soul, to treat every blessing as if it were not quite as good as she was accustomed to. But her words fell on heedless ears. Every one was intent on the littlest warrior.

Close on the time of sunset, Run-all-day joined his people about the fires. " The colour has come back to his face," he said.

" She is a good doctor, that old woman," said Green Bow, nodding. " I am glad you found her alive, chief."

CHAPTER VII

BRIGHT ROBE FINDS HIS ENEMY

Now it happened that Bright Robe, having wandered to the vicinity of Great Devil's Lake after months of fruitless searching for Wise-as-a-she-wolf, saw Run-all-day, in his waving spruce-branches, flying eastward from the hillside. Of course he thought it was his rival, Wise-as-a-she-wolf.

" He flies with the feathers, not the moccasins," he muttered, gazing after the grotesque and fast-vanishing figure. " Has he not enough magic to make himself invisible? Or has he forgotten that I have returned to my country? " he added, viciously.

Knowing that it would be useless for him to try to follow the speeding figure, even to keep it in sight, he bent his steps toward that part of the hillside from which he had seen his supposed enemy rise into the air. After a hard climb through the half-melted drifts, he arrived at the lodge of Whispering Grass and found the old woman still crouched by the fire.

" Why have you come back? " she asked, without looking up. " Have you spilled the medicine? "

" It is not Wise-as-a-she-wolf, to whom you speak," said the visitor. " It is Bright Robe."

She raised her head and stared at him intently. " And does the great Bright Robe, the defier of the gods, come to poor Whispering Grass for medicine? " she asked.

" Nay, I want none of your mixtures, old woman," he replied, slipping into the lodge. " But I would know where Wise-as-a-she-wolf set out for, a little while ago."

The woman smiled secretly, and stirred the pot by the fire. She knew something of the history of both the magicians.

" If that was Wise-as-a-she-wolf, he goes northward," she said.

" I saw him flying eastward, old woman," cried the magician. " It is breath wasted that is employed in lying to Bright Robe," he added sternly.

" Flying? " she queried.

" You need not pretend to doubt it," answered

the man. " He flew like a hawk — for the red feathers were in his moccasins. And he flew eastward, across the lake. Had I seen him sooner, an arrow would have caught up with him, I think."

" Why did you not fly after him, great chief? " she asked. His face darkened with anger and his eyes glowed like coals in the dusk of the wigwam.

" He has both the moccasins of the wind and the red feathers," he replied, harshly. " He travels like a bird while I toil along the ground; and yet, let me but stand within fifty strides of him and I shall crush him as a child crushes a nut," he added, furiously.

" Is not your power great enough to wing your own feet with magic? " asked Whispering Grass, shrewdly.

Bright Robe stepped forward, overturned the pot of medicine with his foot, and then hurried from the lodge. He did not take the trouble to draw his robe above his head and vanish, but stalked across the clearing, slowly and disdainfully.

Whispering Grass snatched a bow and an arrow from the corner and hobbled after the magician, muttering between tears and curses. She caught the gleam of his robe between the dark trees;

but, even as she drew the bow, he turned and saw her. Quick as thought, he pulled the magic robe high and stepped aside. In the next instant, the arrow struck the trunk of a fir-tree, and stood quivering in the wood.

" In truth, it was the great magician," cried the old woman, trembling with fear, and peering anxiously about. He had vanished quicker than the shifting of a sunbeam. She knew that her doom was sealed. A hundred stories of the cruelty of Bright Robe, told to her when she was a child, awoke in her mind. Not once, during his age-long life, had he been known to forgive an injury.

Next moment, with awful suddenness the magician reappeared, close beside her. His face was that of a devil. He let his silver robe fall from his shoulders and raised his club high.

There sounded a swishing in the air, close above them. Then, with a fierce, shrill cry, Bright Robe sprang aside, whirling his club around him so swiftly that it drew gray circles in the sunlight. At the same moment, he snatched for the silver fur which lay on the ground. Twice he lifted a corner of it, and twice it was pulled away from him by some invisible hand. Rage shone in his face like a fire, and horrible sounds escaped from his lips.

The old woman managed to crawl to the edge of the wood; and there she crouched, sobbing with terror and yet unable to remove her gaze from the frantic scene. She realized that the cruel magician had been attacked by some invisible power even while his club was raised to kill her and that now he fought a terrific battle, handicapped by not being able to see his antagonist. Her eyes and brain were keen, but her body was numb; and so she continued to crouch, with the bow still held in one withered hand.

At last the robe of white fur skin vanished from the ground. Its owner dashed here and there in the sun-lit clearing, roaring like a wounded animal and slashing the air with his club. Suddenly he halted, listening, then, with a shrill scream, he dashed toward the tree in which stood the arrow Whispering Grass had shot at him. But before he had crossed half the intervening space, the arrow vanished from the tree trunk. Turning short, with a movement so powerful and quick as to seem scarcely human, he sprang toward the old woman. Almost in the same instant of time the bow was snatched from her hand, apparently into empty air. At sight of that, Bright Robe threw himself flat on the sodden snow, his great body shook and dwindled, — and behold, a slim, white hare darted from the empty clearing into the forest.

An hour passed. The old woman crawled to her wigwam and squatted in the doorway. Several times she heard a strange noise in the air, as of a swift small wind. But the tree tops were not stirred by it. The flames of the little fire behind her sank and the coals faded to black and gray. The sun stood midway in the southern sky, and cast a straight shaft of light through the smoke-hole in the roof of the lodge. But Whispering Grass gave no heed to either the fire or the sun, but gazed out, eager yet fearful, for more wonders to be enacted in the quiet clearing.

The sun slid a hand's breadth to the westward and the shaft of light ran crooked in the dusk of the lodge. A tumult of crashing branches arose on the upper slopes of the hill and descended toward the clearing. Out of the shelter broke Bright Robe, now in his human form, but many times increased in stature, struggling with and clinging to some unseen body in his arms. His club was gone and blood ran down his great breast from a gash in the shoulder. He put his gigantic muscles to every trick of wrestling, showing no fatigue, and yet he was forced backward and downward, and sometimes swung almost clear of the ground. Sweat streamed from his great face, and stood like dew on his body, from which his shirt of dressed leather had been torn.

The desperate battle wrenched and twisted half-way down the clearing. There, for a dozen seconds, it paused, as if the strength of the invisible one had slackened. Then, with redoubled violence, Bright Robe was forced backward again, flung from side to side, battered, staggered, and overborne. Now his face, for the first time, shone with the pitiful, inner illumination of fear. He screamed in his anguish of spirit and bent all his strength to clear himself from the grasp of the invisible enemy. He hurled his gigantic body this way and that, dragging backwards and sideways. Half-grown trees were snapped off by the straining feet of the wrestlers. Blood dyed the trampled snow, — more blood than that which ran from Bright Robe's wound. At last, beyond the fringe of trees at the lower edge of the clearing, the evil magician fell, crashing, to the ground. A scream of fear and baffled passion clanged across the wilderness, ringing from wood to wood and waking terrific echoes against every hillside. For a little while there continued a sound of gigantic struggling.

Whispering Grass was still squatting on the threshold of her lodge, when a young man issued from the woods where the fight had so lately ended, and limped toward her. His clothing of fine white leather, set out with bright stones, was torn and blood-stained. Blood streamed down across his face and breast from a gash on his forehead. Even the moccasins on his feet were torn and dyed with blood. The sight of his pitiful condition drove the numbness of fear from the old woman and she hobbled forward and helped him into the lodge and onto her own couch of spruce branches and furs.

" I am in sore need of your healing, Whispering Grass," said the youth, faintly.

" Lie quiet," she replied. " In a few days you will be able to tell me how you came by these grievous hurts."

But her curiosity pricked her shrewdly to know if this young man had been mixed in the terrific battle, part of which she had so lately witnessed.

And did he know anything of the Unseen One who had vanquished Bright Robe? She washed the wounds on the stranger's head and breast, and bound them with dried leaves of medicinal virtue. She gave him a draught that was both vivifying and soothing. He was already nodding when she removed the torn coverings from his feet, to attend to the cuts and bruises thereon that puzzled her even more than the hurts on his body. His eyes flashed open.

"Give me the moccasins," he cried, eagerly, extending a hand.

"I will make you a new pair," she said. "These are past mending."

"Not so," he replied. "Give them to me, I pray you. Place them under my head."

She humoured him, smiling the while at his foolishness. Within a minute, his eyes were closed in slumber.

CHAPTER VIII

THE YOUTH RECOVERS HIS STRENGTH AND VISITS
RUN-ALL-DAY

WHEN the young man awoke after a sleep of
sixteen hours' duration, he begged for food.
Whispering Grass held a small vessel of broth to
his lips. He drained it at a gulp, and demanded
meat and fish.

" I am hungry," he said, "for I have spilled
blood and the strength of an hundred men. Do
you expect me to recover my lost energy by means
of a mouthful of hot water?"

Much against her convictions as a physician,
the old woman cut a meagre slice of dried caribou
meat, broiled it and gave it to the invalid. He
devoured it ravenously, making no more than two
mouthfuls of it.

" You will heat your blood. You will have a
fever," she exclaimed.

" My friend," he replied, " this is no time for
half-measures. Even my good hunger belt would

be useless now. Though you behold but a small man lying here, sorely cut and bruised, yet the strength of a giant must be recuperated."

" Of a giant? " she queried, wondering if the fever had already found him.

He nodded. " Of the giant who mastered Bright Robe," he said.

" Of the great, invisible one? " she asked, in an awestricken whisper.

".Even so. Was it not a great battle? "

" And you — ? Why must you eat, young man, to feed his body? "

" We have but the one mouth, old woman," he replied, smiling gently.

" Who are you, chief? " she cried.

" They call me Wise-as-a-she-wolf," he said.

Whispering Grass was amazed and disconcerted. For a long time she could do nothing but gaze at the slight, mild-featured youth reclining on her couch. Could this be the furious, invisible fighter who had hunted the mighty Bright Robe from one form to another before her eyes; who had done battle with him, struck fear into his heart, and overthrown him?

At last she found the use of her tongue again. " You saved me from his wrath, chief; but who is to protect me when you go again about your great affairs? " she asked.

" The heart of Bright Robe is known over all the world," she continued, " and his black soul is never deaf to the cry of vengeance. When the winds forget to blow we may expect that terrible one to forget those who have angered him."

" We shall be warmed by five summers before Bright Robe regains his power to harm," replied the youth. " For five summers and five aching winters, he must make his home in the trees, in the shape of a little brown owl."

" Why did you not kill him, chief? " asked Whispering Grass. " He is your enemy, and the enemy of the whole world."

" I did what was in my power," replied Wise-as-a-she-wolf. " Only the gods can take his life. He and I have drunk of the same river, that flows around and around at the very top of the world. But I took his magic robe from him, and broke his giant's body, and spilled his magic for five winters. He could have done no more to me had he defeated me in the battle."

" And when the five winters are sped? " queried the old woman.

" I shall be waiting for him," replied the youth.

The wounds of the good magician healed with a wonderful rapidity, that was not entirely due to the skill of Whispering Grass. And his appetite for food, for a few days, was a thing to strike consternation to the heart of a housekeeper. He ate dried fish and dried meat like a pack of wolves, for a giant as tall as a pine and as broad as a hill lurked within his slender frame. He promised that he would refill the larder as soon as he was on his feet.

On the third day after the battle, he was able to sit up and repair his moccasins, which had been torn on rocks and timber in the heroic combat. They had not been made for such rough usage, for they were the moccasins of the wind. While he worked, patching and stitching with skill and patience, Whispering Grass told him of the visit of the chief who had come for medicine for his child, and of how Bright Robe had seen him flying from the hillside and had mistaken him for Wise-as-a-she-wolf. She described the chief; and the magician knew that Run-all-day had made use of the red feathers.

On the morning of the fifth day after the fight with Bright Robe, the youth arranged his garments of dressed leather, which had been cleaned and mended, and assured the old woman that his injuries were entirely cured and that he must go about his business again.

"It was a speedy cure," replied Whispering Grass. "I can find the wish, in my selfish old heart, that your magic and my poor washes had not healed the wounds so quickly, for now I shall spend my lonely days in fear of that little brown owl."

At that the youth laughed. "Only the mice and the sparrows need fear him, for many moons," said he.

"But the heart within his little breast is still the heart of Bright Robe," argued the old woman, dismally wagging her head.

"I tell you that he is harmless, save to the smallest creatures of the wood," replied the magician, with a note of sternness in his voice. He stepped to the door of the lodge.

"I shall return in a few minutes with meat and fish and pemmican," he said.

Then, for a second, she heard the swishing rush of his flight. She hobbled to the doorway and looked out; but the sky was empty. So she turned back and busied herself with setting the lodge in order, muttering and shaking her gray head over the wonders that had crowded, of late, into her secluded life. She was spreading the skins on the couches when a shadow fell across the floor. Turning, she beheld Wise-as-a-she-wolf. His smooth face was flushed and he breathed as one after a sharp run. "Your storehouse is full," he said. "I went to my own village and got food for you; enough of the best to last you three moons. And here is a little whistle, made of willow. Blow upon it if you happen to be in need of my help, and I shall hear, and make speed to you, no matter in what part of the world I may be. But remember, should you blow upon this whistle without real need, the note of it will not reach my ears."

The old woman accepted the gift gratefully and immediately set about fastening it around her neck by a leathern thong. And when she raised her eyes from the task the good magician was gone.

Wise-as-a-she-wolf, invisible by the potency of his own magic and with the silver robe of his rival under his arm, sped eastward in search of Run-all-day's village. The afternoon was well spent before he found it, for it was a new village.

Alighting nearby, under a clump of crowded pines, he hid the white robe and walked, in his usual form, through the woods to the clustered lodges. Half a dozen women, and a few old men, were seated outside the wigwams, some weaving rough baskets and others laboriously shaping canoe paddles by means of flint wedges and knives. They looked at the strange young man with undisguised wonder. He greeted them good-naturedly and walked straight to the big lodge, feeling sure that, in so small a village, Run-all-day would be chief. Singing Bird caught sight of him before he reached the open doorway and whispered to Red Willow that the young man who had spent a night with them, during the previous summer, was approaching. Then Red Willow and old Blowing Fog knew that it was the great magician. Run-all-day and the other able-bodied men and boys of the village were away, hunting the beaver and musquash along the breaking streams.

Wise-as-a-she-wolf, great in magic, fearless in battle, peeped into the lodge. On seeing only women and children there, he stepped shyly to one side and looked vaguely around, as if uncertain what to do next. The chatter of women could not be answered by magic and his valour was no shield against the big eyes of

Singing Bird. But before he could plan a dignified escape Red Willow looked out and invited him to enter. He stepped cautiously within; whereupon she sent all the children save the baby to play outside, thus making room for him to sit on one of the skin-covered couches. He inquired the whereabouts of Run-all-day, and then asked if the baby was quite recovered from its recent illness.

"He is cured, chief, thanks to your gift of red feathers," replied Red Willow.

The magician expressed his pleasure at this and smiled bashfully at the baby. Then followed a silence that lasted for several minutes. It was broken by old Blowing Fog who had been blinking curiously at the visitor ever since his arrival.

"Great magicians were bigger men, in my young days," said she.

Red Willow and Singing Bird were horrified at that remark; but the young man laughed good-naturedly.

"There was Highest Star, who slew the great moose that swam across the Narrow Sea," continued the old woman, complacently. "He killed the fearful beast with one blow of his closed hand. Many a time did he visit my father's lodge. He was ten feet high and broad as a bear is long."

" And where is he now?" asked the youth.

Blowing Fog could not tell him, for certain, but she had her suspicions. One was that the gods had grown jealous of his greatness and had buried him under a mountain. Another was that he himself had become a divinity and now sat in some gorgeous lodge beyond the sunset, superior to the affairs of the island in which he had been born.

" Nay, do not mourn him," said the youth, " for he still lives on the earth and is even now in this island."

" Then I would I might see him again," cried Blowing Fog, " for he was as beautiful and good as he was big."

" Highest Star was one of the names men called me by," said the magician, modestly.

" But he was double the size of you, chief," expostulated Blowing Fog. " With one blow of his hand he killed the great moose that swam across the Narrow Sea to overthrow our lodges."

She eyed him skeptically.

Wise-as-a-she-wolf nodded his head. " Yes, yes, I remember," he said. " The great moose was thrice the size of his kind and his antlers spread more than the width of this fine lodge. He was king of all the moose of the western lands. But I was more than ten feet high when I slew him. Large as I was then, I doubled my stature before I encountered that gigantic beast. As he drew himself out of the water, I smote him on the forehead, for the safety of my people."

"Then why do you go about in so humble a shape to-day?" asked Blowing Fog, cunningly.

"You do not believe me," he said, eyeing her steadily.

The old woman was silent for a moment.

"Even Bright Robe stood in fear of Highest Star," she said, "but Wise-as-a-she-wolf went softly about the world, studying magic. He was not a great warrior."

"Highest Star was one of the names men called me by," replied the youth, quietly. He looked at Red Willow.

"Do you doubt what I tell?" he asked her.

"I do not doubt you, chief," she replied.

At that moment the voice of Run-all-day was heard without, speaking to Singing Bird. As he entered, the women turned their eyes from the magician to the door.

" Where is the great and good Wise-as-a-she-wolf? " asked the hunter, peering about him. Sure enough, there was not a sign of the young man in the lodge.

" He is here," whispered Red Willow. " He was seated there, but a moment ago."

Blowing Fog gazed wildly around, but said nothing. She trembled with fear, and wished that she had not voiced her doubts nor spoken slightingly of the gentle ways of Wise-as-a-she-wolf.

" I do not see him," said the hunter. " Surely he slipped outside when you were not watching."

He gazed all around, and up and down. " Was he angry? " he asked. " Was he displeased with me for having used the red feathers? "

" You used them in a good cause, my friend," said a gruff but kindly voice from up near the peak of the high lodge. The three stared upward, awe-stricken. The old woman clung desperately to Red Willow. At last Run-all-day found his voice.

" Are you displeased with me, chief? " he asked.

" Nay, friend," replied the voice of the unseen, from the dusky peak of the lodge, " 'tis Blowing Fog who has displeased me with her talk."

"But she is old, chief," said the hunter, apologetically. "Her wits are dull, but her tongue wags. I am sure that, whatever she said, she meant nothing disrespectful by it."

At that, Blowing Fog loosed her hold of Red Willow's hand, and, forgetting her fear, glared in rage and amazement at her tactless son-in-law. So she wagged her tongue, did she? And she was old? And her wits were dull, — the impudent rascal. She drew a deep breath, preparatory to loosing her wrath upon the hunter, when the voice from the roof spoke again.

"I, too, am old," said the voice. "I was old before this woman was born; and yet I do not doubt a person's word until I have proved him a liar."

The hunter looked sternly at the old woman. "You doubted this great chief's word," he cried. "And yet you know that it was by his magic gift that I was able to fly to Whispering Grass, and home again, swift as a hawk, and so save the life of the little warrior."

Blowing Fog was now too angry and mortified to fear anything.

"Silence, blockhead!" she cried. "What do you know of magic and magicians? 'Tis but a little while since you were afraid to touch the red feathers. And Bright Robe turned your heart to water, with a glance."

She looked upward. " Chief," she said, " have you but made yourself invisible and thrown your voice into the peak of the roof, or do you really stand with your feet on the ground and your head in the smoke-hole? "

Poor Red Willow was horrified at her mother's temerity and uncalled-for rudeness. With a sobbing cry, she tried to place her hand over the old woman's mouth. But she did not succeed, and received a shrewd blow on the cheek for her pains.

" Old woman, you shall see, with your own eyes, whether or not Wise-as-a-she-wolf speaks the truth," cried the angry voice from above.

" Forgive her, chief. Do not hurt her," cried Red Willow and the hunter. Then they fell back, against the bark walls of the lodge, speechless; for there bulked a great figure, its feet in the middle of the floor, its knees bent, and its head against the very top of the roof.

" These quarters cramp me," said the giant, and he immediately straightened his knees and his back and expanded his chest. The great lodge was ripped and torn, and with the top of it on his head, the incensed magician strode away into the woods.

Then there was panic and tumult in the village. Women screamed and men shouted and old Blowing Fog fell down in a fit. Red Willow clutched her littlest baby tightly in her arms and her other children scampered to her protection and clung to her garments.

"Silence!" cried Run-all-day to the villagers. "I do not blame the great magician for getting angry and showing his power. And see, he has hurt no one. Throw some cold water on the old woman. She insulted my friend and master in my own lodge — and yet we must not let her die in the grip of fear." He was very angry with his mother-in-law.

Liberal sousings of icy water soon caused the old woman to open her eyes, spring to her feet and attack the people who had carried the water and poured it upon her with such gusto. She dealt old Green Bow a slap on the side of the head that shook the few teeth in his jaws, and was about to assault another ancient warrior when Wise-as-a-she-wolf, once more in the shape of a mild young man, again appeared. At sight of him she slipped quietly behind the fattest person present. The magician went straight to Red Willow.

"I am sorry that I lost my temper," he said, sincerely. "I acted like a braggart; and I have ruined your fine lodge. But I will set to work immediately to rebuild it."

The poles and bark of which the big wigwam had been constructed were uninjured. Wise-as-a-she-wolf and Run-all-day set to work like beavers and their example was soon followed by all the villagers save Green Bow. He, poor old man, went home and nursed his jaw. By the fall of dusk the big lodge was as good as new again, and the entire family and their guest sat comfortably within. Blowing Fog busied herself with cooking the evening meal, and had not a word to say. But the sight of Wise-as-a-she-wolf's stature and strength had impressed her tough old heart more than a dozen less spectacular demonstrations of his magical powers would have done.

The good magician, his conscience still pricking him for his recent violence, made himself very agreeable. He cut several of the bright stones from his shirt of leather and gave one to each of the children, including the girl, Singing Bird, and the littlest baby. "They are jewels of courage," he said, " and impart their virtue to the wearer. They were dug from great mountains, by a fierce red-skinned people who live far to the south and west, in a great land beyond the seas."

He told them some of the adventures that had befallen him since their last meeting. He gave a modest account of his battle with Bright Robe, near the lodge of Whispering Grass. The heart of Run-all-day was glad within him when he heard that the cruel magician had been overthrown and shorn of his powers for five long summers. Even Blowing Fog forgot her disgrace for a moment and cackled. " Ho! ho! Think of that little brown owl with the heart of that great magician under his ribs. He will be a mighty slayer of wood mice. Ho! ho!"

Everybody laughed at that, — even the little children who did not know what it meant.

Early next morning the magician drew Run-all-day aside and charged him to be careful of the red feathers.

" Make use of them only in worthy adventures, for the saving of your own life or the lives of others," he said. " And do not let them become a matter of common report, for even though Bright Robe is harmless for a long time, there are many others who know their virtue and would risk much to possess them. Remember that you have them in charge for the littlest warrior, of whom I expect great things."

Then he went into the woods and took the white robe from its hiding-place, and flew northward and westward.

CHAPTER IX

THE LITTLE BROWN OWL HUNTS FOR FOOD

WISE-AS-A-SHE-WOLF had not been gone from the clearing of Whispering Grass more than ten minutes before the little brown owl that had once been Bright Robe made his appearance from the gloom of the woods and perched on one of the poles at the peak of the lodge. The old woman looked up and saw the round, yellow eyes staring down at her with such a hateful glare that she knew them for the orbs of the cruel magician. Her heart weakened within her. She could not remove her eyes from the threatening, baleful regard. But as the owl did not come nearer, courage returned to her by slow degrees. She remembered that, no matter how murderous the bird's designs upon her, he was but a bird after all, with no power to change his shape until five long summers were passed. So, suddenly, she turned away, snatched a fagot from the ground and hurled it upward through the smoke-hole in the peak of the wigwam. But the owl was already in the air, floating back to the dense shades of the forest.

The owl did not move again from his retreat in a thicket of pines, until night. He was hungry; and as soon as darkness fell he ventured from his perch to look for food. The thought of raw flesh was not repulsive to him, for he had even eaten it in his human form; but he had grave misgivings as to his present ability to kill. He knew that he must fly very quietly, peering about for mice and birds, and, at the first movement in the moss or foliage, pounce down and strike with his claws. So shrewdly did hunger gnaw him that he quite forgot, for the time being, the indignity of his position.

He moved through the forest ways like a drifting shadow, sometimes close to the ground, sometimes among the pointed tree tops. For several hours he hunted high and low, far and wide, without detecting so much as a sign of life in woodland or barren. At last he lit on the tip of a little spruce tree and peered sharply about on all sides and listened intently. He heard a slight rustle at the foot of the tree but could see nothing. Again the rustling sound came to his alert ears and he saw something moving on the ground, beyond the lowest branch of the tree. It must be a mouse he thought, and the idea fairly made his little beak water with anticipation of the feast.

He marked the spot, and pounced. His claws hooked into a hairy mass. Something snarled and sprang. With a terrified squawk he bounced to one side, just out of reach of a pair of snapping jaws, and flew swiftly into the top of a pine. He had mistaken the tail of a fox for a mouse.

The owl learned several more useful lessons that night; but he made no kill. He was knocked about by a white hare, on which he had pitched with a magician's scorn of the powers of a hare; but he was only a very small owl after all, and the astonished bunny had dealt him a shrewd blow with one of his big hind legs. The only mouse that he had discovered had escaped him with ease; and, most bitter of all his experiences, he had been hunted himself by a great white bird whose wings were as silent as his own. Just before dawn, he returned to the lodge of Whispering Grass and found a few scraps of frozen fish near the store-house of bark and logs.

He ate these ravenously, tearing them with beak and claws. When his hunger was satisfied, he examined the store-house carefully. It was a very small building, raised on four stumps to a height of several feet from the ground. The walls were made of logs, fitted tightly and strongly together, but it seemed to him that the roof was composed of nothing more substantial than a few sheets of birch bark. He scratched at the bark with his claws and jabbed at it with his beak. He got quite beside himself with rage; but his desperate attempts to tear the roof of the old woman's store-house, so that he could carry away her meat and fish, proved futile.

At last, weary from his exertions, he flew to a near-by tree to think the matter over. He did not care greatly about the food, for its own sake, for a very little of it would keep him in plenty; but he wanted to steal and destroy it so that Whispering Grass would starve. A bright idea occurred to him. He would go to a lynx, or a bear, and tell him that much good food lay close at hand, with only a roof of bark to cover it. And perhaps he could even persuade some big animal to destroy old Whispering Grass herself. Surely the mention of his true name would be enough to induce the fiercest beast in the forest to do his bidding.

The little owl lurked in a tree-top all day, planning his revenge on the old woman. As soon as dusk fell, he flew to the clearing and beheld Whispering Grass squatted in the doorway of her lodge, eating her evening meal. A dish of meat lay on the ground beside her and the smell of it awoke a man's appetite in the stomach of the fluffy little bird. He perched on the top of the lodge and stared down at his enemy and her repast. He made no sound, and she did not look up. Suddenly he dropped upon the dish, sank his claws into the largest slice of meat, flew swiftly back to his tree and swallowed it to the last tough shred.

The old woman knew, in a moment, that the thief was Bright Robe, for no other owl would have sufficient courage to take food from so near a human being.

"He might even attack me," she mumbled, "and claw my eyes out."

So she carried her supper into the lodge, fastened the flap across the doorway and put more wood on the fire. Terror of the evil magician was like a cold wind upon her back.

After finishing his meal, the owl set out in search of a lynx or a bear. The little victory over Whispering Grass made him feel quite like his old self; but he did not forget the lessons that he had learned the night before. He flew cautiously, avoiding the open spaces for fear of the big white bird. He investigated every thicket, entering from above as a matter of discretion. Though he was looking for a lynx, he did not want to find one unexpectedly, and he suspected the lower branches of every tree of sheltering a crouching fox.

After several hours of searching, the little brown owl happened upon an old she bear. She was hunting mice and seemed to be in a cranky humour; and when the owl accosted her politely, in the language of the woods-people with which he had become familiar during his long life as a magician, she did not so much as look up at him. The owl was nettled.

" Do you hear me speak? " he asked.

The bear grunted and began to amble away.

" Hold, hold," cried the owl. " If you are hungry, I can tell you where to get food in plenty."

At that the bear halted and turned.

" Hungry," she grumbled. " Would I be grabbing at little mice if I were not hungry, you miserable, fleshless bunch of feathers? "

" If you talk like that," replied the owl, " you may go fill your paunch with moss and twigs."

The bear grumbled more than ever. She did not like owls, for they had the reputation of pretending to know a great deal, and, in reality, of knowing very little. Also, she had once tried to make a meal off one of these scrawny birds, in a time of famine. On the other hand, she was far too hungry to turn her back on any chance of obtaining a full meal.

" You must excuse my rudeness," she grumbled, " but I'm really so worried about the scarcity of fish and soft roots and the activity of the hares, that I scarcely know what I say. I believe you mentioned food. What kind of food? "

" Pemmican and smoked salmon and dried caribou meat," said the owl.

The old bear sat up and pressed her paws to her stomach.

" If I could only believe it. But you owls are all liars," she mumbled.

" I only appear to be an owl," said the little bird. " I am, in reality, the great magician Bright Robe."

The bear paid no attention to this remark.

" Where is the food? " she asked.

" In the clearing of that old woman called Whispering Grass," the owl informed her.

" In her store-house? "

" Yes."

" And is the old woman dead? "

" No," replied the owl. " She is not dead yet."

" Perhaps you mean that you intend to kill her," sneered the bear.

" If you carry away her food, then she'll die of starvation," said the wicked little owl.

The bear was quite inarticulate with fury and disgust. She ran to the tree on which the bird was perched and clawed at and shook it.

" You feather-head," she managed to growl, at last, " do you want me to get my hair all eaten off again by that old woman's red fire? I know her store-house, you rascal. It is as strong as a rock. I tried to break into it once, when I was younger, and she came out with a stick of fire and hit me a hundred times."

Before the owl could recover himself from the unexpected outburst of wrath, the old she bear had ambled swiftly into the depths of the forest.

CHAPTER X

THE LITTLE BROWN OWL HAS MORE TROUBLE

THE little brown owl was both astonished and enraged at the bear's behaviour. He wanted to cry threats and derision after her; but he had already learned that it is not wise for a small owl to make itself too conspicuous in the wilderness, especially at night. So he contented himself with planning, for a full half-hour, the fate of that she bear, should she oblige him by living until the five long summers and winters of his enchantment were passed. Even in his pitiful bird-shape he enjoyed nothing so much as the scheming of awful revenges on his enemies. So for awhile, the matter of the old woman was driven from his thoughts; but it was recalled to his mind by the sight of a lynx moving noiselessly past the foot of the tree upon which he was perched. Without hesitation, he requested the big cat to stop and hear what he had to say. The lynx obeyed like a flash, leaping into the air and alighting with his head toward the tree, crouched, his green eyes sinister and steady.

" Who speaks? " he snarled.

His round head was close to the ground, much lower than his hind-quarters, under which his great hind legs were doubled like springs. He was ready to launch himself upward or forward, as the case might require. His white teeth gleamed in the starlight.

" It is I, Bright Robe, who speaks," replied the owl. The name seemed to convey no particular meaning to the lynx.

" Hah, it is nothing but a little owl," he snarled, and turned about as if to continue on his interrupted business.

" Not so fast," cried the other. " I am Bright Robe, the great magician, the greatest magician in the world."

" I have no time to sit and listen to the lies of an owl. I am hungry and must hunt," replied the big cat.

" I tell you, I am Bright Robe, the master of magic," cried the bird.

" Then turn yourself into a nice fat hare, and jump down here, and I'll turn you into a lynx," said the beast, grinning wickedly over his shoulder.

" I am something of a magician myself," he added.

" Why do you not believe me? " asked the owl.

" Who ever believed an owl? " replied the other, " or, for that matter, who ever believed the word of Bright Robe? So you are a liar, whoever you are."

The owl changed the subject immediately.

" If you are looking for food," he said, " I know where there is plenty of it."

" What kind of food? " inquired the lynx.

" Pemmican, and smoked fish, and dried meat," replied the bird, in his most seductive voice.

" Nothing fresh? " asked the other.

" Well, not fresh, exactly, but all sweet and in prime condition."

" Where is it? "

" In the storehouse of old Whispering Grass."

" Miserable bird," cried the lynx, " why have you wasted my time with this idle tale? That old woman's store-house is as strong as a pine-tree."

" The walls may be strong," replied the owl, " but the roof is of bark. One stroke of your great claws would tear it to strips."

" It was of poles, laid snug together, when I last clawed at it," said the lynx.

" I tried it last night," answered the owl, " and it was of bark."

The lynx came close to the tree and glared up at the bird. His eyes were round and green, and made the owl feel quite uncomfortable. He was glad that Wise-as-a-she-wolf had not let him loose in the wilderness in the form of a hare.

" Why are you so anxious that I should have plenty of food? " inquired the lynx, suspiciously. " I did not know that we were such good friends."

" To be honest with you," replied the owl, " I want you to eat and carry away the old woman's food so that she shall starve. My suggestion is not prompted by friendship for you so much as by my enmity toward her."

" How is that? I never knew the old woman to have an enemy before," said the lynx.

Then the owl told the story of how the old woman had shot the arrow at him, when he was in his proper form of Bright Robe.

" Why did you not slay her then, oh mighty one? " sneered the lynx, who did not believe a word of the story.

"It — it was not convenient for me to do so, just then," answered the bird.

"Then why not do it now?" asked the lynx. "If you are a great magician 'twould be a simple matter for you to turn yourself into a bear and go tear the old woman's store-house to fragments, or even eat the old woman."

"To do so now would disturb my plans," cried the bird, petulantly. "I do not wish the old woman to see my hand in the matter," he added, more quietly.

The big cat snarled disgustedly.

"Why do you tell me such a foolish story?" he asked. "I have never heard so many lies in all my life before."

"It is the truth," said the bird.

"I don't know why a miserable little owl should want an old woman to starve (which she wouldn't, anyway, because she can catch plenty of fish in the lake), but I'll just go along and see if what you say about the roof of the store-house is true or not," said the lynx, turning and walking away.

The owl flew after him and floated above his head.

"I did not think of that," he said. "I forgot

that she could catch fish in the lake. You had better go right into her lodge and kill her."

That was too much for the lynx. Without any warning, he sprang into the air and struck at the bird with unsheathed claws. He missed his mark by an inch.

The terrified owl flew into the nearest tree and sat there quietly for half an hour. He was thoroughly disheartened, and could not help wondering what would have happened to him if the lynx had struck him. Of course he would have suffered the pangs of a violent death; but would his spirit — his immortal life — have remained in the body of the great cat, after it had crunched and swallowed his meagre flesh and bones, or would he have been fated to wander, formless, until the awful five summers were passed? The idea was a terrible one, however he considered it. As a man, even as a magician, he had always feared pain; and, surely, it was better to be a bird than have no body at all.

At last the little owl roused himself from his unpleasant reflections and winged silently away in the direction of the lodge of Whispering Grass. He soon reached the little clearing, and floated across it, close to the ground. He alit on a small tree in the shadow of the woods, from which he had a good view of the lodge and the store-house. He had not been perched there long before he saw the lynx steal into the starlit clearing from the black edge of the forest. He was not surprised at the sight.

The lynx advanced cautiously, slowly, often halting and looking suspiciously about him. He circled the lodge twice, then crept to the store-house and glided around and around it. He evidently suspected the owl of trying to tempt him into a trap. At last he stood up on his hind legs and clawed the walls of the little store-house inquiringly. He sniffed at the cracks between the poles, at first with distrust but soon with evident relish. He reached up a paw and felt the roof of bark. He examined it, in this way, from all sides, and failed to detect any manner of trap. At last he dropped back, squatted for a moment, and then sprang lightly to the roof and straightway began ripping the bark. At first he did it gently, inquiringly, but soon, finding a stout protection of poles everywhere under the bark, he became violent. The fragrance of the pemmican and fish and flesh stole up to his hungry nostrils and he forgot all caution in his mad efforts to tear the well-pinned roof into fragments.

The owl, watching from his perch, was at first surprised at the other's failure, then amused. The roof was more substantial than he had thought, after all. Well, it did not matter (except to the lynx), since the old woman could live by catching fish in the lake.

The great hide which hung in front of the doorway of the lodge was drawn noiselessly aside; and neither the owl nor the toiling lynx noticed it. Then, suddenly, there sounded the sharp twang of a released bow-string, and, with a snarling scream, the lynx sprang from the roof of the store-house and fled into the woods. Again the bow-string twanged and a second arrow sped from the black interior of the wigwam. It struck a glancing blow on the roof where the lynx had so lately stood, flew upwards and sideways and hit the unsuspecting owl a hard blow across the breast with its shaft.

The owl found himself on the ground, feeling very sore and ill. He tried to fly, but could only flutter a foot or two at a time, so bruised were his muscles. He knew that the ground was not a safe place for him and immediately began to

make violent efforts to get into a tree. Again
and again he hopped and fluttered, only to fall
back each time as if the boughs of the little spruce
had pushed him away. It was not only discouraging, but it hurt; and, worst of all, he still remained on the ground, at the mercy of prowling
animals. He rested for awhile, and then continued his painful efforts to get into the tree.
Failure followed failure, and he was steadily
loosing strength. He had about decided to give
up the attempt and look for some sort of hole in
which to hide when he heard a soft foot-fall behind him. In a frenzy of terror he hopped upward again, flapped his wings desperately, touched
the end of a branch about six feet from the ground
and clung with beak and claws. He felt himself
slipping back. He clawed; he threshed the air
and branches with his sore wings; and, at last,
he reached a solid perch. At the same moment
a big red fox glided, like a shadow, under the
tree. That was a close shave for the little owl.

CHAPTER XI

THE MAGIC LODGE

Of all the great magicians in the north, Wise-as-a-she-wolf alone worked solely for the welfare of mankind; and, as his reputation for virtue grew, so did his enemies multiply. But, with the exception of Bright Robe, not one of them could compare with him for cleverness, or courage, or knowledge of the secret arts. Few of them possessed either brain or determination enough to master more than the simplest lessons in magic. Having attained so far, they were content to practise their little arts covertly, to serve their own ambitions. They overthrew their enemies by provoking stronger people against them, working slyly, with many false tales and foolish antics. They had been at the bottom of most of the wars in the big island, and, though they seldom fought in the front of the battle (not possessing the mastery over death, as did Bright

Robe and Wise-as-a-she-wolf), yet they usually gained power and wealth at the cost of the warriors' lives.

These people hated Wise-as-a-she-wolf, because he had always worked against them. When he was at home, the island was at peace; but no sooner was it known that he had gone to some distant land than a dozen little wars sprang up, every village was turned against its neighbour and battle and starvation ravaged the country. But, of late years, the island had been quiet and prosperous. Bright Robe had been so long in exile that he had become little more than a figure of legend, and Wise-as-a-she-wolf had spent enough of his time in the island to keep the designers of evil in constant fear. Then the news of Bright Robe's return, in all his old power and wickedness, reached the little magicians. They heard that he was intent on the overthrow of Wise-as-a-she-wolf, and at that their black hearts rejoiced, and they began to plan murders and battles and thefts on their enemies. A few of them had even seen Bright Robe and offered him their services; and he was as great and terrible as their fathers had told them. And then, of a sudden, he had disappeared and they feared that their wicked master had deserted them, and had offended the gods afresh.

Now, with Bright Robe again reduced to a term of inactivity, the good magician had time to devote himself to an important task of a rather more private nature than that of keeping his countrymen in order; and this was the building of a stronghold in a forest in the very heart of the island. This forest was fenced, on the south and west, by a bend of the Purple Hills. Northward and eastward of it lay trackless marshes and naked barrens. The forest was of pine trees for the most part, standing tall and thick over miles of gently rolling country; and in the centre of it lay a pond, fed by hidden springs of pure, ice-cold water. The good magician's lodge stood beside this pond. He had commenced it when he first began to learn magic, and year by year he had worked at it; and still it was not entirely finished. There was ever some new beauty to be added to roof or walls. Only the Crimson Wigwam, beyond the western edge of the world, and other homes of the gods beyond the walls of ice, surpassed this magic lodge which Wise-as-a-she-wolf had built with his own brains and hands. To begin with, one might stare straight at it for hours, or for a hundred years, and see nothing but pine trees. There was not so much as a sign of a clearing to lead one to think that a great lodge stood there. And yet, if one were able to reach that particular portion of forest where the lodge was, and pass the walls, he would find that he could walk straight through the tree trunks, as if they were as immaterial as shafts of sunlight. And so they were. For the sturdy pines that seemed to crowd so close in the compass of the lodge were but images of the trees that had stood there before the magician had cut them down, spellbound there to deceive the common eye. Nothing but the greatest magic could have accomplished such a miracle. But the builder had guarded against the chance of any one blundering against the invisible walls and thereby discovering their magic quality, by encircling the immediate vicinity with enchantment so potent that it would lead a traveller ever to one side or the other and yet let him believe that he was walking straight ahead.

This forest was occasionally visited by wandering hunters, and more than one party of adventurous braves had camped, for a night or

two, beside the crystal pond; but none had ever
suspected that Wise-as-a-she-wolf's home was
so near at hand.

To eyes that could see it, the lodge was a fas-
cinating and beautiful place. Every stone, and
log and sheet of bark that had been used in the
building of it, had been converted, inside or out,
into something rare and wonderful. Bark had
been taken from a thousand birch trees and half
as many fir trees to cover the roof, which was
higher than the top of the tallest pine and painted
like the roof of the world; painted so cunningly,
with magic pigments, that it changed in colour,
hour by hour through the days and the nights
and the seasons, with all the colours of the sky.
It was as beautiful as the sky; and yet neither
rain nor snow could pierce it, and clouds could
not hide its charms from the dweller beneath it.
At night it shone with stars, made of rare jewels
which the builder had brought from a distant
land. They flashed an hundred colours in the
light which shone from the big lamps in golden
vessels that gave forth no smoke in the burning.

The outer walls (invisible to the eyes of every
one but Wise-as-a-she-wolf) were dull and plain,
save for the windows of crystal as clear as ice.

They were built of great fragments of granite, and pine logs, set skilfully and firmly together. But within, the rough materials had been smoothed to fine surfaces whereon the master had painted hunters and beasts, warriors, lovers and battles, spring and summer and winter, children and gods, in living colours. Never had there been such a picture before; and never, I fear, will there be such an one again. He had wrought on it for years. To stand in the midst of those four walls was to have life, and all the men and wonders of the world, within the glance of your eye. Here stood two young lovers in a sunlit glade; and there sat a group of old story-tellers around a cooking-fire. Here a hunter stooped above a fallen stag, his red knife in one hand, his slackened bow in the other; and there a young mother washed her babe in a clear stream. Here a god stood huge and black against a sunset sky, looking out across a darkening world of pigmy villages and wide forests; here a naked child sat in the sunlight and played with toys of carved wood; here were fields of ice, and a gray sea, and innumerable seals; and there ran a great wolf with his thin red tongue hanging from his jaws. Here was a girl weaving a basket of split willows, her face bent demurely above her work; and you had but to turn your head to behold five-score warriors in battle, dealing blows and shedding blood.

As these pictures grew under the hand of the good magician, it seemed to him a pity — great work selfishly done — if no one but himself should be allowed to enjoy them. So he went out from his magic house, and travelled among his people with this thought in his mind. And, first of all, he found a man called Wounded Hawk, who was crippled and sick and a burden to the village in which he lived. The man was tired of life, for he had always been active and adventurous, and now his hunting days were over because of an injury he had received in a fight with a bear. So the magician took him from his poor wigwam, in the dead of night, and carried him to his own magic lodge.

For twenty days, Wounded Hawk lived in that house of wonder; and not once, in that time, did he see his unknown host, though food and drink were always at his hand. He lived as one in a dream, and was happy from dawn till dark in the contemplation of the pictures, all valour and romance and tenderness and adventure and sheer delight; and yet he knew that they were but drawings of a real world and common things. So his old zest in life returned to him, and his face grew rosier and his eyes brighter. Stories of the battles and the huntings and the homelier incidents, stirred in his brain. On the night of the twentieth day, as he lay in a sound sleep, Wise-as-a-she-wolf lifted him in his arms and carried him back to his poor wigwam. When he awoke, he looked about him at the sloping walls of bark and rubbed his eyes. Then he laughed, thinking of the wonderful dream he had enjoyed and of the pleasure he would have in telling it to his friends. Though he was still lame in one leg, he felt vigorous and happy, and left his lodge and greeted his friends with a merry face.

Of course they stared at him in amazement. "Where have you been?" they cried. "You look as if you had found a good hunting-ground."

"I have had a good sleep, and a fine dream," replied Wounded Hawk.

"Have you been sleeping ever since you went away?" they asked. "Have you been dreaming for twenty days?"

"Twenty days?" queried Wounded Hawk, opening his eyes wide.

" Did you think that we would not look inside your wigwam, when we missed you? " asked the chief of the village. " Come, now, tell us what mischief you were about? "

Wounded Hawk shouted with joy. " Then it must be true," he cried, " and not a dream after all."

They continued to question him, and he told them a little part of the wonder of the magic lodge and magic pictures. At first they thought he was deceiving them; then they crowded about him to hear his stories. They built him a comfortable lodge and gave him furs and food; and his fame went abroad as the master of story tellers, the maddest of dreamers.

And from then, to the day of his death, life seemed a fine thing to him and the world a delightful place. The wonders of the pictures and the magic lodge were always green in his memory and his stories carried the fame of the Pictures of Life far and wide. Warriors and children came to his lodge and begged him to talk, and he told them great stories. He even painted pictures, with coloured earths and dyes, on bark and dressed hide, making them as much like the pictures in his mind as he was able. And he was always striving to make them better, and to tell finer stories. Love and honour were his; and when he died, people mourned him as the mightiest warrior is not mourned. And his soul (which was not crippled) went gladly out on an eternal quest of valorous and beautiful things.

Another had seen the magic lodge. An old woman, whom the good magician had found in a deserted camp, had ended her days there, thinking herself beyond the black river of death.

CHAPTER XII

THE ADVENTURE OF JUMPING WOLF

JUMPING WOLF was a young man of twenty years of age, who belonged to a big village in the south. His father had been chief of the village until an enemy — a coward who knew a little magic — had first worked his downfall by secret methods, and then killed him with his own hand. Then Jumping Wolf killed the murderer with a blow of his club, knocked three of the false villagers senselesss, and ran for his life. That happened in March, when the snow still lay deep, but with a crust over it in most places.

Twenty men, old and young and of middle-age, gave hot chase to Jumping Wolf. They filled the woods with their cries of anger; but the fugitive ran quietly, saving his breath and his strength. He was a good runner, and had been named for his agility. Within a half-hour of the fight in the village, five of the oldest men gave up the pursuit and leaned heavily against the trunks of trees,

gasping for breath. They felt so many pains in
their insides from the unwonted exertions, that
they were sorry they had left the village. It was
not long before more of the pursuers stopped
running; and they were so spent that they
simply fell flat on the snow, in agonies of ex-
haustion. They were very fat, and wondered
why they had been such fools as to join the chase.

Within an hour of the commencement of the
flight, only four men continued to run on the
trail of Jumping Wolf. These were strong men,
tireless and courageous. Two of them were
seasoned warriors and two were youths of the
fugitive's age. At last the chase led to an open
barren which, after a mile of level, sloped up to a
bleak hill. Here and there on the barren were
ponds and great boulders, and clumps of spruce-
tuck.

Jumping Wolf headed straight across the barren,
running evenly and steadily; and, as he ran, he
slipped his bow from his shoulder and pulled an
arrow from the quiver at his belt. He had done
nothing but slay the murderer of his good father,
and there was neither relenting nor fear in his
heart. His had been the hand of justice; and if
he must die for it he would die fighting. Death

was nothing for a man to fear — but, life? — ah, it was surely a pleasant state. So he fitted the notch of an arrow on the string of his bow, and ran on until he reached a little clump of spruce-tuck. Here he turned, breathing deep. One of his pursuers was already half-way across the intervening open and the other three were clear of the woods.

"Go back," shouted Jumping Wolf.

But the warrior who led the chase paid no heed to the warning. Then Jumping Wolf raised his bow, pulled the notch of the arrow back to his ear and let the shaft fly. It struck at the feet of the leading pursuer, piercing the crust and bringing the warrior to a standstill.

"Go back," shouted Jumping Wolf, again. This time the enemy obeyed. Turning quickly, he ran back and joined his companions.

At that they all halted and looked uncertainly toward their quarry, across the white expanse of snow. One of them carried a spear and the others clubs or knives; but none of them had bows or arrows. They did not know what to do next, and stood there, panting and staring. They had not counted on finding the young man so formidably armed, for his club had been knocked from his hand during the fight in the village and they had not seen, during the long run through the woods, the bow on his back.

Jumping Wolf stepped forward six paces.

"There is no mercy in my heart," he cried, and again raised his bow, with an arrow fitted to the string. "You have hunted me like a lone wolf, now feel how long and sharp are the fangs of Jumping Wolf," he shouted, and loosed the shaft. They dodged this way and that; but one of them stumbled, leaped up again and scooted into the forest with a flake of sharpened flint sunk in the muscles of his shoulder. Next moment, another felt the pang of a wound in the flesh of his leg; and the young man laughed fiercely to see the barren so suddenly cleared of his enemies.

As only four arrows remained in his quiver, he retraced his steps to where the first arrow stood upright in the crust and returned it among its fellows. Then, after a keen scrutiny of the forest woods into which his enemies had retired, he turned again and continued his journey across the barren and up the side of the bleak hill. He looked back, from the ridge of the hill, but could detect no sign of his late pursuers. Before him lay more barren ground, and beyond that the black forests stretching on every side. He looked up at the sun, a silver ball in a sky of March blue.

" I shall go east and south," he said, and went forward bravely. He felt no ill effect from the desperate run he had been forced to make. But grief and anger, and hate for the village that had been his home, glowed in his heart.

So he travelled for days; and, for a time, he spent his nights without the cheerful company of fire, not sure that his enemies had left his trail. He killed enough small game to supply himself with food, and suffered from nothing except loneliness, and sorrow for his father's death. He had known no other care save a father's since his earliest years. On the tenth day after his escape from the village, he wounded a young stag with his arrows and then ran it down in the melting snow. So he built a small shelter where the stag was killed, and paused in his journey to make a pair of snow-shoes, and smoke some of the meat.

In this manner he spent more than a week very comfortably. When the snow-shoes were made, and the best parts of the meat were cured, and a dozen blunt-headed arrows shaped, for the killing of partridges and hares, he set out again on his journey.

By this time, the soft voices of spring were awake in the wilderness, — the murmur of streams gnawing at rotten ice, the dull creakings of subsiding snows, the swish of thawing winds across the miles of forest. The snow was wet and heavy, where it still lay deep in drifted places, and Jumping Wolf was glad that he had halted to make the snow-shoes, rough as they were.

The spring advanced swiftly. Soon the streams were roaring free and the great rivers were swinging the pans of broken ice in mid-current; boiling over them, and driving them together, mass upon mass, in tumbled barriers of white and gray. The lakes and ponds moved in their depths at the sure call, split the roofs of their prisons, and sent the sullen fragments adrift.

The shades of night were gathering through the forest, and Jumping Wolf was beginning to look about him for a suitable place to camp when an arrow whistled past him, close to his head. He sprang aside, into the shelter of a tree trunk, and peered back along the way he had come. His keen sight detected a movement, as of a shadow, slipping among shadows. He unslung his bow

from his shoulder, and in so doing was reminded
of the fact that his snow-shoes, crude, heavy
affairs, still hung over his back, where he had been
carrying them since the previous day. He was
about to free himself from their weight, the better
to flee or fight, as the case might be, but he
stayed his hand. He might need them. Anyway, he was pressed for time, now.

He still possessed five barbed arrows. He
drew one of these, placed the notch on the string,
and slipped the blunted arrows on the ground.
Then he stood motionless, watching and listening.
A small stream, swollen with snow-water, ran
somewhere near at hand, and he could hear no
sound save its gurgling and booming. After a long
suspense he saw, by the faint light, the figure of
a man stealing toward him. He waited, alert
and breathless, until it came so near that he knew
it for the warrior at whose feet he had shot the
arrow into the crust, on the first day of his flight.
Then, without a word of warning, with the rage
of a hunted beast in his heart, he drew the bow
and loosed the shaft. The warrior uttered a
piercing scream, sprang forward and fell on his
face.

Jumping Wolf ran, keeping straight to his course

through the twilight forest. He had heard cries of rage in answer to the scream of the wounded pursuer, and another arrow had passed near him; but now, save for an occasional swish of underbrush on his track, the hunters made no sound. He ran steadily, but with care, for the ground was treacherous. Beyond the bow and four remaining arrows, he was unarmed. He had not even the flint blade with which he was in the habit of preparing his meat for cooking. The knife had dropped from his belt, unnoticed, early in the day. He had not so much as a well-balanced stick, with which to fight at close quarters.

Presently the ground began to slant before him. He slackened his pace a little and ran more cautiously; and the pursuit drew nearer. Now the slope became very marked, and twice, in the thickening darkness, he stumbled heavily. But friendly underbrush saved him from falling. His face and body were switched painfully by branches and he bruised his feet on roots and rocks.

Suddenly, through the dark wood in front, he saw a glimmer of open spaces, a gray glimmer dotted with lighter spots, and in another second he stood at the edge of a great lake whose farther

shores were hidden in the night. Pans of ice
dotted the grim water for as far as he could see,
and one, of good proportions, swung within sixteen feet of the shore.

He had been well named when the chief, his
father, had called him Jumping Wolf. Without
a moment's hesitation he retreated a few paces,
then ran forward to the lip of the cold tide and
leaped into the air. And even as he alighted on
the raft of ice, on feet and hands, with bent knees
under him, he felt something strike and glance
from the snow-shoes on his back. He had been
saved from the flinthead of an arrow.

The shock of contact drove the ice-pan, sullenly rocking, farther away from shore. Jumping
Wolf steadied himself for a second, crouched
low. An arrow struck the ice close to his hand;
another zipped into the water a few feet beyond.
He turned, still crouched low, and loosed his
remaining arrows, in quick succession, at the
black shadows. A sharp cry and more arrows
answered him. Two of the shafts struck ringing
on the ice, and glanced across into the water.
He removed his snow-shoes from his back, bound
them firmly together, face to face, lay flat as near
one edge of the pan as he dared, and used them

for a paddle. The unwieldy craft answered to the strokes, circling and wallowing, but drawing steadily away from the dangerous shore. He paddled with all his strength, and once narrowly escaped pulling himself into the water. Now the arrows flew wider, and he knew that his enemies were judging his position, and the distance, without the help of their eyes. He was already congratulating himself on his temporary escape, when a shock and pang numbed his wrist. With a groan, he lost his hold on the improvised paddle. One of the chance arrows had found him out.

The jagged flint had torn an ugly wound in his wrist, which bled freely; and the pain of it, for a time, was bewildering. His belt was of soft leather, and with this he bound the wound securely, tying the bandage with a spare bow-string. After awhile he began feeling about, in the darkness, for his snow-shoes. He probed here and there, on every side, with his bow; but they had either sunk, with the weight of raw-hide thongs, or drifted out of reach.

It was cold out on the swollen, ice-drifted lake; and it grew colder and colder as the hours passed. The night was black and clouded, without so much as the glint of a star in the sky. A chill wind was afoot, driving the ice-pans down the lake.

Poor Jumping Wolf found himself in a very discouraging situation. His right arm from finger tips to shoulder throbbed steadily with the pain of his hurt. Cold bit every bone and hunger gnawed at his stomach; and the desolation of this strange, black lake, the extent and name of which were both unknown to him, got into his soul. But he would not give up the fight, or even so much as contemplate despair. He had travelled so far, and made three such brave escapes from his enemies, that he could not believe the end of his career was at hand. So he kept on his feet, constantly shifting backward and forward a few steps each way, and waving his uninjured arm about to keep his blood in circulation. His great hope was that the pan on which he stood would be driven to the shore by daylight, or that the ice would be massed sufficiently close to allow him to gain the shore by leaping from cake to cake. He knew that, in his condition, weakened from cold and loss of blood, it would be sure death to attempt a swim of any distance in that icy water.

The night dragged out its black length. The

wind fell; and by the time a lift of gray dawn showed in the east, Jumping Wolf was crouching on the ice, fighting an awful weariness and craving for sleep that weighed on brain, eyes, and limbs. But as the light strengthened, he raised his head and looked about him. He saw, with a dull disgust (for he was almost past caring) that the shores were far away and the ice-pans drifting wide apart. He staggered to his feet and gazed around. Was that a trail of smoke above the dark trees? If so, perhaps it was from the camp-fire of his enemies. But smoke meant fire, and fire seemed the very spirit of life to his chilled brain. He should like to see that fire, to get close to it, even if death were the price. He could not per-suade himself that death was to be escaped, in any case; so he sent a shrill cry ringing across the water. Next instant he tottered, and fell within a finger's-breadth of the edge of the pan. Horror of the icy colourless flood sickened him, and he crawled back to safety and lay quiet.

CHAPTER XIII

THE cry from the lake was heard by Run-all-day and other early risers in the little village. It was also heard by Jumping Wolf's enemies, who had camped, for the night, on the other side of the lake. But they could not answer it, for they had no canoes.

Run-all-day looked in the direction of the cry and detected the human figure on the distant ice-pan. He saw it fall, move slightly, and then lie quiet. He lifted his great canoe of bark, which, fortunately, he had repaired with resin the day before, in preparation for the spring journey, and carried it to the shore. He shouted for his paddle; and, in a moment, Singing Bird came running from the lodge, with two paddles on her shoulder. She, too, had seen and heard the sufferer out on the drifting ice.

" Let me go with you, and paddle in the bow," she begged.

As the water was smooth and the ice scattered, the chief nodded his permission. In another second the great canoe was in the water and the white paddles were plying and flashing.

At last the canoe slid softly alongside the pan of ice on which the stranger lay, face-downward.

" Come, friend. We will give you a softer bed than that," cried Run-all-day.

The young man stirred slightly, but did not raise his head. The bow of the canoe was within a few feet of him; so the girl leaned forward and prodded him sharply with her paddle.

" Harder! Harder!" cried the chief. " If we do not wake him now, perhaps he may never wake. Look, there is blood on the ice."

Singing Bird reached out again and jabbed the stranger's ribs with determination but inconsiderable force. At the third jab, he drew himself up on his knees and looked at them with a wide but dim glance. He gazed at the chief and then at the girl.

" I do not know you," he said, slowly. " You are not from my village. Why did you hunt me so? "

" We are your friends, lad, and we did not

hunt you," replied Run-all-day. "Crawl over here and get into the canoe."

The young man did as he was told, but in a dazed, half-hearted manner.

"Steady," cried the chief. "Don't step on the gunwale. There now, lie down."

Then Singing Bird pushed the bow of the canoe away from the flat ice-pan with its great, red stain of blood. She wondered what the stranger's story would be, and her young heart fluttered at the adventure; but she paddled none the less diligently for all that.

Silently crouched in the cover of the woods, the men who had so recently been in murderous pursuit of Jumping Wolf beheld the rescue of their quarry. They were six in number; for, after Jumping Wolf's first stand against them on the barren, they had returned to the village for reinforcements, carrying their wounded. They had taken up the chase again, with a strong party, urged to the deed by the brother of the dabbler in magic who had slain the old chief and who had been slain, in turn, by Jumping Wolf. But this worthy brother had not joined in the long chase himself. It was wiser and more comfortable to sit at home and plan new campaigns. Now the

pursuers were tired of the hunting. They had
lost their bravest man by Jumping Wolf's arrow,
the night before. Another had been wounded.
They were in a strange country and longed for
their own lodges and cooking-fires. So, when
they saw the great canoe put out from the oppo-
site shore, and the rescue of their intended victim
from the ice, they retreated cautiously and then
faced southward and westward for their own
country.

Jumping Wolf lay in a raging fever for days.
More than once his feet were at the very edge of
the long, dark trail which leads, at last, to the
hunting grounds beyond the setting sun. But
he was well nursed, in a quiet lodge, by old Blowing Fog and Singing Bird. Red Willow brewed
herb-waters for him, when she could spare the
time from her babies; and all the old men and
women in the village gave medical advice, which
Blowing Fog told them to keep for their own
ailments. The commencement of the northward
journey was delayed for two weeks by the
stranger's illness, for Run-all-day would not risk
the life he had saved for so small a matter as an
early settlement in their summer lodges. But
some of the cod-fishers grumbled, and even

talked of parting from the other villagers and going about their affairs without the sanction of their chief.

" Go, if you wish," said Run-all-day. " But if you do, you need not return to this snug village when the frost comes. You will have to find another chief then, and another hunting ground, and build new lodges."

After all, they reflected, Run-all-day was a mighty warrior, a friend of magicians. Also, the valley was warm for a winter camp, and the surrounding forests were rich with game. So they agreed that it was better to lose a few codfish than their membership in the village and the protection of their big chief.

When the fever had burned itself out of Jumping Wolf's brain and the awful weights and pains had passed from his chest, he told his story to his new friends. No one doubted a word of the tale. Run-all-day was so moved to anger against the distant villagers, that, had his awe of the red feathers been less, he would have put them within his moccasins and flown southward, to strike terror into those treacherous hearts. But, as it was, he vowed that Jumping Wolf had his love and protection for as long as he wanted them.

" Let me be one of your people, chief," said
the young man. " You waked me from the awful
sleep, gave me care and medicine, and turned my
feet from the long trail. Only my own father
and my mother, when I was a small baby, ever
showed me such love as you and your people
have shown me. When I am strong again I will
hunt and fight for you and your house."

So Jumping Wolf, the fugitive from the south,
became a warrior of Run-all-day's little clan.

The water was still high in the lakes and rivers,
but clear of ice, when Run-all-day and his people
at last set out on the northward journey. Now
the days were warm, and the willows were bursting their silver buds. The alders were fragrant
with yellow blossoms. The snow had faded
away, save from the darkest recesses of the
forest, and many furtive blooms shone from the
moss that floored the woodland valleys. Geese
and duck and brant had returned to their northern
breeding-places; plover and snipe piped and
flew, and the burnished kingfisher flashed along
the river, from point to point, grinding out dis-
cordant warnings, at the approach of the canoes.

They travelled swiftly, though forced to make
many portages by the strength of the swollen

water. It was Run-all-day's intention to go all
the way to the great bay of salt water into which
the River of Three Fires runs, making his summer
camp there so as to keep his village intact. He
was proud of his chieftainship. A greater and
not less honest ambition than to kill salmon
was astir in his manly heart. He dreamed of
a strong clan, mighty in peace and in battle,
with himself as its head and the friendship of
Wise-as-a-she-wolf for its protection. He knew
that the future held great adventures; that a
day of reckoning must come between the evil and
the honest in every part of the island. He knew
that Wise-as-a-she-wolf was the enemy of every
worker of evil, and he knew that this meant that
every other magician in the land, great or small,
was the secret enemy of his friend and master.
Never before had Run-all-day called a man his
master, even in his thoughts; but his brave and
steadfast heart had gone out to the good magician. He would fight his master's battles, when
need came, and he would see that his people did
not shirk the fray.

He told his ambition to Red Willow, who was
not in the least displeased with it. She did not
think her husband uncommonly clever, but she

was sure that he was wise; and wisdom is a finer thing than nimbleness of wit.

" I shall not be the least of my family," said Run-all-day. " The world shall hear of me as a warrior and chief. I will care for my people as I care for my family; and there will be talk of my name around the cooking-fires long after my bones have been covered with the heavy stones."

" You plan too far ahead, chief," cried Red Willow, tenderly. " Let us not contemplate the talk of the villages, an hundred summers hence."

On the third evening the whole party camped about a mile above the great falls. There would be a long carry, next morning, around that roaring, smoking tumult of black rocks and white waters. By the clear, early light they would drop down, keeping close to the shore, to a point as near the top of the falls as they dared. But now, with the twilight deepening every moment, it was safer to land well out of reach of the torn currents. The chief's canoe had leaked slightly during the day; so, while the others made camp, he unloaded it and repaired it with the mixture of melted fat and gum which he had invented for the purpose.

Very early next morning, before the elders

were astir, two of the chief's little boys, one of
eight years of age and the other of six, stole from
their beds to play. No day was long enough for
playtime, so they must begin at the breaking of
dawn. They ran over to their father's big canoe.
It lay with its bow at the edge of the water,
empty. They played about it for a few minutes,
jumping in and out, and sometimes pretending to paddle, each with a little stick. It was
not long, however, before the elder of the two
began shoving at the stern of the canoe. The six-
year-old joined him in the good work. What was
the fun of playing ashore when the river lay so
near? Now was the time to put pretence away and
voyage forth like full-fledged warriors. The
canoe touched the water — advanced into the
current inch by inch. Now half its length was
afloat and the black water tugging at it. The
children pushed and heaved, strong with the
fire of adventure. They were helped by a current
that slanted outward from the shore at this
point, turned toward mid-stream by an eddy
just below. At last the canoe slipped free, and
the children scrambled aboard with a shout of
delight; and the slanting current laid hold of the
bark and swung it gaily away.

Old Green Bow, attracted by their shout of glee, was the first to discover the children's danger. He saw the great canoe, riding high on the water, swing in mid-stream and speed down the racing river. He saw the little heads above the gunwale, and the little arms dipping the sticks over-side, as if they would hasten the canoe on her course to the churning falls below. Green Bow's wits were hopelessly muddled at the sight. He stared, open-mouthed and blank with horror. Then he ran to the edge of the shore and waved his arms frantically and foolishly after the speeding craft. At last a shrill cry broke from him.

When Run-all-day saw what the matter was, his tanned face went pale as the bark of the distant canoe. Uttering a low cry, he sprang for one of the heavy skin-covered boats of his followers, and began unloading it with desperate energy. Even as he worked, the canoe bearing the children rounded a wooded bend and flashed from sight. He was about to hurl the skin-covered craft into the current, still half loaded, when Red Willow touched his arm.

" Quick! Here are the red feathers," she cried.

He slipped them into his moccasins, snatched a paddle from the ground, and leaped into the air; and the clustered villagers shouted as he rushed through space and beyond their sight, like a great bird. He did not follow the river, but slanted upward and passed over the wooded bluff 'round which the canoe, with its precious freight, had so lately disappeared. He marked it again in an instant, in a sweep of his vision, still unwrecked, but dashing, unsteered, where the water flung itself into white crests against a thousand scattered boulders. The roar of the falls was in his ears, and he saw its crown of spray not half a mile beyond the racing canoe.

He swooped downward and forward, with all the speed of the magic feathers. It was plain to see that no human skill and strength could save the good canoe from that mad tumult, so he loosed hold of the paddle. It fell in the water and swirled away. Next moment he was low above the canoe. His flying feet touched the trembling structure. Close ahead spouted a fountain of white water. The children were lying flat on their faces, sobbing in an agony of fear. He snatched one, then the other, to his breast and let the doomed canoe go from under his feet. He rose a little distance, clasping his children firmly, and watched the canoe fling itself into the white water, emerge bottom-up and swing on, a battered wreck, toward the hungry falls. He had not been a second too soon. He uttered a loud cry of thanksgiving, turned, and set his feet strongly to the currents of the morning air. And when the villagers saw him top the wooded point, with his double burden, they shouted again, and danced wildly with up-flung arms.

CHAPTER XIV

THE GOOD MAGICIAN VISITS RUN-ALL-DAY'S NEW VILLAGE

THE "carry" around the falls was accomplished by noon. Fifteen miles farther down stream was another dangerous place, not a fall, but a long rapid that no canoe could get through at high water. That passed, it would be quiet voyaging down to the great bay.

Run-all-day did not utter a regret at the loss of his fine, birch-bark canoe, though it caused quite a disturbance and delay in the arrangements of the party. Well below the falls, in a grove of pines that stood close to the river, the men set to work to cut logs for a raft. They used fire and their axes to fell the trees. It was a slow job and a hard one. When the trees came down (which they did not seem in any hurry to do) the branches were hacked off, and then the trunks were divided into as many logs of the required length and girth as they contained.

Everybody worked willingly, for even the laziest of the young men realized that the favour of a great chief like Run-all-day was well worth sweating for. He was a friend of the good magician; he possessed the power of flight like a bird; he was able to snatch his children — then why not his warriors? — from the very jaws of death. So they hacked and burned with a will.

At last ten logs were ready and rolled down to a quiet eddy against the shore. Six were floated side by side, close together, and bound firmly with thongs of hide. The other four, slightly smaller in size, were bound on top of the six, making a sort of upper deck which stood clear of the water. But by the time the raft was completed, the sun was so low in the west that it was hardly worth while to embark again that day.

Next morning the raft was loaded with the provisions and household goods that had begun the journey in the lost canoe. Some other freight was added, and Run-all-day's family found seats, here and there, in the other canoes. Then the chief and one of the young men manned the raft, one standing at each end, and pushed it out of the eddy with long poles. The raft proved almost as swift, or, rather, not much slower than the canoes of hide, and it was certainly a great deal steadier and as easily managed. And so they continued their journey, but little the worse for the accident.

When the rapid was reached the raft, with its freight securely fastened, was lowered from eddy to eddy, by means of a tow-line of twisted hide.

Salt water was reached about mid-afternoon of the next day, and the cod-fishers led the party straight to the site of their last year's camp. Temporary shelters were pitched before dark. Then Run-all-day examined the ground on every side, deciding the positions of the lodges and other weighty matters. So, in a week's time, Run-all-day's summer village was built; and the cod-fishing prospered amazingly.

Jumping Wolf won back his strength and was soon able to work at the fishing, to handle the cranky canoes, and to compete with the other men at all manner of sports. At shooting an arrow far and straight, only the chief himself was the new clansman's superior. When he was fully recovered from his illness, he could out-leap them all, jumping either high or wide. Also, he was the swiftest runner in the village; and even in the long races of five miles or more, only the chief could pass him. So Jumping Wolf stood high among the warriors of the little clan.

During the summer, six more families joined Run-all-day's band. They were all of his own people, of the same great tribe into which he had been born. They had been without a leader for several seasons, moving as the whim suggested, hunting or fishing when need drove them to it, and constantly being bullied or robbed by more united families. So, when they heard of the new chief and the new clan, and distorted versions of his flights through the air, they came to him, group by group, and begged to be taken under his protection.

Now Run-all-day, so short a time before content to be only a good provider for his family, found his hands full of other people's duties and his steady head fairly buzzing with affairs. But he worked cheerfully, turning aside from nothing; but when a matter seemed too deep for him he sought the counsel of Red Willow, and usually got wise advice. He fished as diligently as the most energetic of his followers. He trained them in the uses of all manner of weapons, both for the chase and war. He made them practise archery, and spear-throwing, and the art of attack and defence with clubs and knives. He set the old people to making shields of hide and wood; and on rainy days every warrior had to make arrows and bows, spears and paddles. And if any man sulked or idled, the chief took him aside and talked to him, and one such conversation proved enough, in every case.

One August evening, the good magician, Wise-as-a-she-wolf, stepped into the village and greeted the people pleasantly. They had neither seen nor heard of him since early spring. He was in his customary form, that of a gentle, rather under-sized youth. The chief welcomed him with respectful warmth and led him straightway to the evening meal. When all had eaten, a great fire was built at the seaward edge of the village, and around this gathered the warriors and old men. The magician and Run-all-day sat side by side, on a bear-skin, separated a little on either hand from the others.

Wise-as-a-she-wolf spoke first. He had read the story of the chief's ambition at a glance, and praised the village, the clean lodges, and the store of fish. He warned the company against greed, false pride, and deceit, and told them that their hope for future happiness and ever-increasing strength lay in their loyalty to their leader.

" I have seen many a clan torn and scattered from within," he said. " Harbour no traitors or cowards among you, and give ear to no talk that you would not repeat openly to your chief and the whole village."

Then Run-all-day told him, quietly, of how he had used the red feathers again, to save the lives of two of his children from the fierce hunger of the river.

" You did well, friend," replied the youth. " By every noble and merciful deed in which they are employed their virtue is increased."

He bent close to the chief. " They would scarce lift me above the ground, when I last took them from Bright Robe," he whispered.

The story of Jumping Wolf's flight from the south was told by Run-all-day. The magician listened intently, and then questioned the young warrior closely.

" I know those people," he said. " They listen to evil counsellors, to weaklings and cowards who play with magic and work it to their evil desires."

" There is one such coward the less, now," said Jumping Wolf.

" Do not boast of the spilling of blood," replied the magician, gravely.

At that the young warrior hung his head, for the eyes of the great one were upon him.

" But some blood is better on the ground than in the heart," added Wise-as-a-she-wolf, gently. " And of such was the blood of the traitor who died at your hand."

Then Jumping Wolf lifted his head again and looked fearlessly at his companions. His heart was warm with courage, though it had quaked but a moment ago.

As the night advanced, the warriors felt more at their ease. Stories of the day's work were told, and nods and laughter went 'round the circle. More wood was heaped on the fire and old Green Bow, warmed to the marrow, told boastful stories of his deeds in the chase, of what a mighty fellow he was before the years stiffened his limbs. Other old men raised their voices, some to cast discredit on Green Bow's tales and some to sing the glories of their own past. There was talk of battles, and of cod-fishing, and of the killing of seals on the ice-floes from the north.

The magician listened, smiling often, sometimes laughing outright, like a boy: and, thus encouraged, the old men spurred their imaginations to the uttermost.

At last the fire was allowed to subside, the company dispersed, and the chief led his guest to a wigwam that stood in the centre of the village.

" This lodge is yours," said the chief. " It has been in readiness for you since spring. And in our winter village we shall build another for your use, chief."

" You treat me well, friend," said the other, touched by the attention.

" Your red feathers have already saved the lives of three of my children," replied Run-all-day. " They brought medicine to the littlest warrior and snatched two others from the river. Also, you have taught me that, with but little more work and courage, a man may care for a whole village as easily as for his own family."

He drew back the flap of caribou skin that covered the doorway of the lodge, and held a torch high with the other hand, so as to cast the light within.

" Enter with me, brother. I would speak on a private matter," said Wise-as-a-she-wolf.

Brother! The chief's heart swelled at the word. The greatest man in the country, perhaps in the whole, wide world, the good magician, the master of men and magic, called him brother. Ah, he could scarce believe that such honour had come to him.

Within the lodge, the visitor laid his hand on the chief's arm and smiled kindly with his wonderful eyes.

" You have done well, Run-all-day," he said. " I would trust you far, for no foolish pride has come to you with new power, and your honesty remains undimmed. The same cannot be said of many warriors of this island, for evil counsellors are ever at work."

" The woman, Red Willow, is cleverer than I, and gives me light 'on many questions," replied the chief, modestly.

The other smiled and nodded his head. He had suspected as much, knowing that the woman possessed a keener mind than her husband, and he liked him the better for telling it. But, in a moment, his face was grave again.

" I have come to you on an important errand," he said. " I want you and Red Willow to promise to give me the littlest warrior."

The chief's breath caught in his throat and it seemed that his heart stood still, for he loved

each of his children as if it were the only one.
A low cry escaped him, and he stared at the
magician with a flicker of fear in his wide eyes.

" Is it too great a sacrifice to make for the good
of the world, and for your friend? " asked the
other, sadly.

" But he is so little," cried Run-all-day. " I
do not understand. What have I done to dis-
please you, chief? "

" You have pleased me in everything," replied
the magician. " Had you not pleased me so well,
I would not ask you for the child. A time of
warfare and disturbance, open and hidden, is
coming. I have read the future, and I know.
True, I could not see clearly, but I saw far. For
a few seasons there shall be quiet, a seeming
quiet, then the smouldering of the evil fires, in a
score of places at first, and suddenly in an hundred
places.   Then my enemies — our enemies —
will gather, and the flames of hate and lust will
burst forth. The powers of the warrior and the
powers of magic will struggle on both sides, many
magicians on the one side and I alone on the other,
and many warriors against a few."

" And what of the child? " asked Run-all-day,
presently, in a voice low with awe.

" He is of honest and courageous parents,"
replied the other. " I would teach him what I
know, so that when the struggle is upon us, we
shall be doubly strong. I would take him to my
lodge, where he would learn the great secrets,
day by day, growing up with a knowledge of
them."

" And shall he have no playtime? " asked the
bewildered father.

" His very lessons will be play for him," replied
the magician, " and he will be safe and happy."

" But would it not be better to wait until he
is a few years older? " asked Run-all-day. " This
is but his second summer. Surely he is too little
to learn the wonders of magic."

" It cannot be later," replied the other. " I
must take him into my care now, before he has
learned to speak a word, or never at all."

" He will fret for his mother," said the chief.

" Nay, for he will remember nothing," said the
magician. " He will not know that he ever lived
elsewhere than in my magic house, until he is
grown to boyhood. He will be nourished and
protected as if he were my own son. And you
may come to him as often as you desire, and he
will know you for his father; but when you are

gone again he will not fret for you, for there is no such thing as heart-ache in my house. Also, his mother may visit him, but only twice in a season. When he is large and wise enough to do the great work for which I would fit him, then shall he be free as I am, to go and come at his pleasure."

"It is wonderful," said Run-all-day. "He would be safe and happy, and great; but what will Red Willow say about it?"

"We shall take her to the lodge to-night, and show her the littlest warrior's play-room," replied Wise-as-a-she-wolf. "And then, when she is there, I shall tell her; then it will be easy for her to understand."

"How will you take her to the magic lodge?" asked the chief.

"You will carry her," replied Wise-as-a-she-wolf.

CHAPTER XV

THE LITTLEST WARRIOR'S GREAT PROSPECTS

RED WILLOW was slim as a girl, and so her weight was but an inconsiderable matter to the arms of the chief. Also, the red feathers seemed to increase the strength of his body as well as give him the power of flight. The magician, with the moccasins of the wind on his feet, ran ahead along the still tides of the air. The chief followed close, bearing his sleeping wife in his arms. Far behind the village lay wrapped in slumber, dreaming of cod-fishing, most likely.

The night was mild, and the flight not far as birds and magicians fly. They alit in the pine forest; and Wise-as-a-she-wolf immediately touched the chief's eyes with his fingers. Then, to the bewildered vision of Run-all-day, a great mass of builded walls loomed from the blackness of the forest, and from it flowed a light that was as sunrise and red evening and moonshine, all in one.

"Hold her gently," whispered the magician, "and follow me close. We shall awake her within, where no sudden fear, nor tremor of strangeness shall touch her."

They walked forward, for a few paces, and a great door swung open in front of them. The chief stepped across the shining threshold, on the heels of his master, without a twinge of distrust or fear; and once inside, he uttered a cry of wonder and delight. At that glad sound, Red Willow awoke, slipped her feet to the floor and gazed about her with joy in her face. The Pictures of Life marched and glowed on the walls; the smokeless lamps burned softly, here and there; and above spread the mimic sky, with silver stars a-twinkle.

But 'twas not alone the beauty of the place that gladdened the hearts of Run-all-day and Red Willow. Joy and peace were in the air, as well as wonder and delight. Here could be no dread of sickness or sharp foreboding of death; here no thought of hunger, or weariness, or heartache; here could lurk no anger; here could arise no unfriendliness or despair.

"I could sit before these pictures for an hundred years," said the chief. "Surely, though I behold drawings of men and things that I have seen, they are more true and wonderful than life. Or are they so bright and clear that they pierce the dimness of my eyes and spirit? Here are the warriors fighting; and though I have seen battles, and spears thrown in anger, never have I seen clearly enough to so behold the good in one man's face and the evil in another's. And surely the honest warriors are about to win a victory. My heart leaps to help them; my hand is ready for the neck of that great fellow with the evil face. Oh, chief, you have wrought marvellously! Never before have I seen so clearly the difference between the good and the wicked among mankind."

"True, true," cried Red Willow. "And see, here are a pair of lovers, beside a little river. How beautiful a thing it is — this love — and how bright it shines in their eyes. And here is an old man mending a snow-shoe, and even that is beautiful."

The magician smiled. "If the old man's face were not a good face, if his eyes were sly and his expression cruel, there would be no beauty in the picture. So these pictures are like the life of the world; but in the battles I have turned most of the evil faces aside. For the picture is clearer than the real battle, for it is compassed in a glance of the eye. A fight in an honest cause is a noble and courageous thing; but to picture it one must pass over much of the lust and pain, or the sight of it would chill the heart of the bravest warrior."

The good magician gave them food to eat and a bright liquor to drink, and the tastes of these were pleasant and strange to their tongues. Then he told Red Willow of what he had dimly seen of the future and of his wishes concerning her baby, even as he had told these things, a few hours before, to the chief.

" He will be happy, I know, in this beautiful place," she said; " but how can I live without him, great chief?"

He talked long with the father and mother, gently and kindly, explaining the great reward that would be theirs, for giving the infant into his care for a few seasons. They knew he would be safe and happy; and that virtue and wisdom would be taught to him, and knowledge of magic that would make him strong to save his people from destruction.

The three returned to the village before dawn. They carried with them some of the wonderful liquor from the magic house, that Red Willow might feed it to the baby, to ascertain whether or no it would agree with him. Wise-as-a-she-wolf had smiled at this precaution, but kindly; and he had made no objection. He remained in the village for seven days, always gentle and helpful and friendly. He worked no deeds of magic and, in outward seeming, was but a modest young man of small stature; and yet he won the hearts of the whole village, even of old Blowing Fog, and the unfaltering trust of Red Willow. And the littlest warrior thrived on the magic drink.

On the seventh night, when all was quiet in the village and the great fire was banked deep with its ashes, the three again set out for the lodge in the pine forest; and this time, Wise-as-a-she-wolf carried the littlest warrior in his arms. The baby slept soundly in that firm and gentle embrace, soaring over hill and river and barren, forest and lake as secure as if he lay on the couch of skins in his father's lodge. Again the chief ran hard on the magician's heels, with Red Willow in his arms. The house of delight was reached without mishap, and again the wooden door swung open and let them in. The smokeless lamps still burned; hunters and lovers and warriors still marched and shone on the walls and in the wide roof the stars continued to glint like splinters of ice. And again the joy of the place lifted the hearts of the parents and gave them courage.

Wise-as-a-she-wolf placed the baby in its mother's arms, gazed down on it with infinite tenderness in his eyes, and softly took it back to his own embrace.

"If I should awake him from his sleep, at this unaccustomed time?" he asked, looking at the mother with a boyish smile.

"He would cry lustily," replied Red Willow. "Oh, chief, it would take me many minutes to quiet him."

"Nay, of what profit is the wisdom I have learned in all my long life, if I cannot shield one little baby from the grief of the night-time?" replied the other.

"Magic and wisdom! Ah, the littlest warrior has not yet learned their power, chief," said Run-all-day. "He would surely lift his voice in protest if the very gods awakened him at this hour."

"Nay," replied the magician, "I think you are wrong. The night-cry of an infant is a cry of dread for the dark hours and the vague fears of danger that lurk about the black places of the world. He feels, when only half-awake, the insecurity of his little life, and cries out for the protection of his parents." He touched the child's face with his finger, shook him gently, and at last disturbed the sweet slumber. And the baby opened its round eyes, stared up at the face above it, and laughed.

"Behold," cried the magician. "Am I not a nurse to be trusted?"

Still carrying the baby, he led the way to the far end of the lodge. Here was a small apartment, dimly lit and hung about with curtains of leather dyed in many soft and beautiful colours. He laid the child gently in a little bed of soft stuffs that were of neither fur nor dressed hide. It stood beside a couch on which was spread the white wolf-skin, that had once belonged to Bright Robe. The three bent above it, listening to the soft breathing of the littlest warrior.

"He sleeps safe," said Wise-as-a-she-wolf. "He has no fear of the night-time, now."

CHAPTER XVI

FURTHER ADVENTURES OF THE LITTLE BROWN OWL

Now what of the little brown owl? We last heard of him, foiled in his sneaking enterprise against Whispering Grass, escaping from the fox with the most desperate and painful efforts. For the whole of the following day he remained hidden among the branches of the little tree; and by night-fall he was able to fly again, though slowly and not without pain. He found hunting a difficult matter for days after the blow from the old woman's arrow, so stiff and sore were his muscles; but a worse matter than this was the enmity of the big lynx, whom he had enticed to the store-house of the herb-doctor. For the lynx, having found a roof of strong poles where he had been told to expect nothing but bark, and having received a painful wound in the side from a flint-headed arrow, now proclaimed the treachery of the little brown owl to every bird and beast of that part of the wilderness.

So the owl that had once been Bright Robe, that great and evil magician, lived in fear of his life, in the very country over which he had so often cast the shadow of his evil deeds. None feared him now save the smallest creatures of the wood; and even they found him to be the least dangerous of all the birds of prey. To hide his identity as that particular owl so widely condemned by the lynx, he was compelled to cease his efforts against Whispering Grass and refrain entirely from telling the story of his great past to the forest creatures. For the word had gone abroad that the *small, brown owl that says it is a great magician, and has no modesty of speech, has been proved a traitor by No-Tail, the lynx, whom it led into a dangerous trap. So beware of the owl that talks overmuch, and lies more than is usual even among such birds. Kill him, if you can, for the credit of the forest.*

With every claw, and tooth, and beak in the country ready to rend him, 'tis small wonder that the little owl was utterly discouraged. It was not safe for him even to exchange a word with another owl, so bitter against him were the birds of his kind for the discredit he had brought upon them. Their reputation for wordiness and untruth was so bad already that they lusted for the blood of the stranger who had made it worse. But, for several days, he escaped the anger of the creatures around him by keeping out of their sight. One twilight-time, however, he was attacked suddenly by an owl of his own size; and, for all the fierce heart in his body, he was knocked about disgracefully. He sought safety in flight, at the first opportunity, and travelled many miles, at his best speed, before his antagonist gave up the chase. He pitched into the top of a bushy tree, to recover his breath and his wits. In his cowardly heart he vowed that every bird and beast within ten miles of that mountain should be slain when he recovered his power. He continued his flight, heading southward, and at last had out-flown the lynx's story; and he found a splendid hunting-ground, and fairly stuffed himself with mice. His evil little brain began to plot and plan again, now that he had the comfortable sensation of food inside him. He remembered people who had been his followers, men after his own heart, scattered about the country. They had often been his tools in past troubles; why should they not serve him again as instruments of destruction and revenge? And now the need of them was greater than ever, for he realized how impotent he was, in his miserable owl-body.

These men whom the enchanted magician remembered, were all small workers of magic, sly, greedy folk without courage or principles, and with but sufficient knowledge of the secret science to enable them to destroy their simpler fellows and pass as great warriors. They could increase, by a little, the strength and deadliness of weapons; blind a man's vision, for a short time, by the flashing of bright stones and mumbling of words, and many such pretty tricks as these. But they were all evil, in various degrees, and looked upon Bright Robe as their master.

The strongest of these, the one most advanced in magic, wickedness, and wealth, was Fang. Fang lived in a big village in the south, and was second in power to the chief. The chief was an honest man, ignorant of any hidden arts, but a wise and a mighty warrior. Bright Robe, the little owl, knew that Fang had been plotting that good chief's destruction for many years. Why should he not join in the wickedness? It would be a beginning, and quite amusing, much more amusing than being beaten and chased by owls. He would whisper cunning advice into Fang's ears, and encourage him with his mighty presence, and there would soon be one honest man the less in the world; and that meant one enemy the less.

The little brown owl spent several days in finding the village in which lived his old friend Fang; and when he came to it, at last, and perched on a near-by tree, he was surprised to find all the inhabitants clustered together, every man talking at the top of his voice and no man listening. He saw Red Eye, Fang's brother, in the middle of the crowd; but Fang and the chief, and the chief's son were not there. He listened to the angry voices and soon learned that the people were trying to divide the chief's and Fang's properties among them, — the lodges and furs, the wampum and weapons and stores of food.

Ah, so the chief had already been settled with. And Fang, too, it would seem. But what of Jumping Wolf, that upright young warrior who had never shown fear or respect? But the matter in hand drove these questions out of his mind, for the time. He listened to Red Eye, whose voice outshrieked all the others.

" My brother's goods are now mine," screamed

Red Eye, " and as the chief's goods became Fang's when he struck the blow, so did they pass to me when he was killed."

The air was filled with shouts of rage and derision. Hands (most of them containing clubs and knives) were brandished on all sides.

" We chased the young man, and were wounded by his arrows," cried a warrior at the edge of the crowd. " Are we to have nothing for our blood and weariness? "

" While you sat at home," bawled another.

" We feared Fang, for we thought him full of magic power, and yet Jumping Wolf killed him with one blow," cried a third.

Then they all surged about Red Eye, shouting like mad men.

" No one fears you," they roared. " The old chief used to treat you like dirt under his moccasins."

Now the little owl saw that Red Eye was inwardly quaking. All his false courage was quenched by the angry faces, as a little fire is quenched by a dash of water.

" Share the goods as you will," he cried, " for I am weary of such ingratitude; " and with that, he made his way quickly from the crowd and entered a lodge. Jeering shouts were hurled after him; even the women were not silent in their scorn, and children capered after him with impertinent whoops and gestures.

The owl did not like the state of affairs in the village at all. Fang had been an apt pupil, and a sure man in an evil enterprise. And behold! he was now less than a shadow among his people. Listen! They reviled his name even while they fought over the division of his goods. One warrior, snatching a skin of pemmican from the storehouse of the departed Fang, proclaimed his satisfaction at Jumping Wolf's escape. The sentiment was favourably received, and repeated on all sides.

" Truly, he did us a good turn," cried one, " when he broke Fang's skull with his club; for Fang would have been a cruel master, for all his fine promises. Now we are free and rich, with two fortunes to share among us. Ah, I am glad that we did not catch the boy while Fang's evil spell was on our hearts and brains."

" And he did but avenge the old chief's death," said another.

" You are full of fair words now," cried an old hag; " but you hunted him out, with clubs and spears. I know the breed; and I think that cub may return, to strike another blow at the murderers of the old wolf."

Men and women ceased their wrangling and looked at the old woman who had spoken, with various emotions depicted on their faces. Some looked ashamed, some afraid, some angry; but all showed uneasiness.

A young woman with a child in her arms laughed shrilly.

" You are for ever trying to frighten us," she cried.

" Jumping Wolf is a warrior," said the old woman, gazing fixedly at one of the men. " He and the chief were the only warriors in this village, — two warriors among a crowd of cowards and traitors."

Her voice became higher and shriller. " You listened to Fang, and thought him a great magician; and you watched him slay your chief with his hidden knife. But, ah! In a second Fang, too, lay dead. Then you hunted the lad; and he turned you back. Again your picked men went on his trail; and again he outwitted you. You saw him taken from the pan of ice, alive, by a strong man and a young girl, in a canoe that was not like your canoes. Then sleep light, oh, warriors, for Jumping Wolf has you in his mind. Sleep light, with your spears and your clubs at your side, for you may taste the heat of his arrows again."

It was quite evident to the owl that the old woman's remarks struck home. Some men scowled; some shook their fists at her; and one commanded her to keep silent. She laughed, long and harshly.

"You should thank me for the warning," she cried. "If you but heed it, it may save you your lives. I warned Fang, for he was my daughter's child, against the evil temptings of that blustering Bright Robe; but his heart was wicked and greedy. And now he is dead. So I warn you to choose an honest chief, though you should have to make a three-days' journey to find one. I warn you to deafen your ears against the wiles of the treacherous Bright Robe, for he is less dangerous as an enemy than as a seeming friend. And, again, I warn you against the son of the chief whom you murdered."

The people were now thoroughly frightened by the woman's free and disrespectful use of the name of Bright Robe. They gazed fearfully about them,

as if expecting that awful magician to leap upon
them from the woods or the sky. He had visited
them several times during the period between
his return from exile and his fight with Wise-as-a-
she-wolf, and of that fight, and its result, they
knew nothing. The children gazed around also,
but with curiosity rather than fear, for they did
not understand the gravity of the situation.
And in so doing, a small boy with a bow in his
hand espied the owl in the tree. With a cry of
delight, he fitted an arrow to the string and let
fly. The shaft rattled among the branches within
a few inches of the bird's head; and the villagers,
looking in that direction, saw something like a
tiny shadow drift away into the forest.

The owl was furious at what he had heard
from the old woman. It seemed that every old
woman was his enemy. If she continued to
preach in that vein, and with Fang dead, the
entire village would be lost to him in but a short
time.

CHAPTER XVII

A BRIEF RETURN TO POWER

THE little brown owl waited in the woods, near the village, until close upon midnight. All was quiet when he at last flew to the lodge to which he had seen Red Eye retire, hours before. He perched on the peak of the lodge, and, cocking his head, brought one yellow eye to bear on the dark interior. Pitch black though it was, he could see dimly.

"Red Eye," he called, guardedly. The words were man-words, but the voice was thin and rasping. He heard a sound of stealthy movements below, within the lodge. Then a voice whispered, "Who speaks my name?"

"It is Bright Robe," replied the owl, still in his owlish voice. But he could not remedy the tone of his voice, no matter how he tried.

"Nay, 'tis not the voice of Bright Robe," returned the man in the lodge.

"I have changed my voice and also my form," said the owl, with wonderful patience for him.

" I am sitting here on the peak of your lodge, waiting to be let in. I am not used to waiting. Listen, and you will not doubt that I am Bright Robe." And he whispered some facts concerning the past life of Red Eye and of his dead brother, Fang.

Red Eye immediately untied the opening of his wigwam, and the owl floated from his perch and drifted inside with a soft murmur of wings. Red Eye closed and fastened the doorway again and then welcomed his visitor with much humility and many great names. He could see nothing but the yellow eyes in the darkness.

" I know all that has happened in the village," said the owl, making good use of his wits and of what he had heared before the boy fired the arrow at him. " I have but just arrived, from the frozen ends of the world," he lied, " and I want food. Give me some raw meat."

Red Eye had the carcass of a hare in the lodge, already skinned, and this he placed on a dish of bark and held toward the yellow eyes, muttering apologies all the while for the unfortunate state of his larder. He explained that his fellow-villagers had threatened him so, that very day, that he was afraid to leave his lodge.

" You need not tell me about it," lied the owl, " for I know as much as you do of the matter, though I was an hundred miles away, at the time."

Then he fell upon the raw carcass, holding it with his claws and tearing with his beak. Red Eye trembled at the sound of the awful feeding.

At last, when he had eaten his fill, the owl spoke again. " Fang is dead," he said. " He struck too soon. I told him to wait until I came again."

There was not a grain of truth in this statement; but Red Eye believed it.

" He thought himself strong enough to overthrow the chief, without my help," continued the owl. " And now? Well, you know what came of it. Let it be a lesson to you, Red Eye."

" I hear you, chief," whined the brother of Fang.

The owl snapped his upper and lower bills together, for the flavour of the meal was still with him. He blinked his yellow eyes and stared at the man more fiercely and roundly than ever. He could see quite well now; but the man could see nothing but the yellow eyes.

" I have been on a long journey," said the owl, " even to the land which lies beyond the last mountain of ice. I travelled with the moccasins of the wind on my feet. Wise-as-a-she-wolf had possession of those wonderful moccasins; but I met that weakling in battle, not long ago, and took them away from him. Also, I turned him into a mouse."

Was there ever such a teller of false tales as the little brown owl? And yet Red Eye believed every word he said, for he was stupid as well as evil. He bowed his head before the yellow eyes and chanted, low in his throat, a song of praise. The owl listened with pleasure, for it was a long time since he had heard anything of the kind addressed to him.

" I talked with my friends, the gods," he continued, presently, " and they were glad of my victory over Wise-as-a-she-wolf. They told me to go about quietly, in the form and manner of an owl, and take note of such as are my friends and still more particularly of such as are my enemies. And in three moon's times, I openly proclaim myself master of this whole island, my enemies shall fall, to the last man, and to the last old woman."

" Hah," gasped Red Eye. " You mean Hot Tongue, great chief? "

"Yes, Hot Tongue, among many," replied the owl. He supposed that Hot Tongue was the old woman whom he had in his mind, at the moment, — the old woman who had spoken so freely of him, that day, — but, however that might be, he must appear to be quite certain of everything.

"Those who prove themselves my friends shall have villages under them, and great stores of furs and food and wampum," he said.

By this time Red Eye was prostrate on the floor of the lodge.

"I have always been faithful to you, great chief," he cried. The owl snapped his beak again. He was sure of Red Eye's stupidity, at any rate.

"Whatever you have been in the past," he said, "I want you to prove your devotion now. This lodge suits me well. You may move into another. And in the morning you may bring me food and water, and later, the warriors of the village. I wish to speak with them."

"I fear that no other lodge will receive me, great chief," whined Red Eye. "Should I stir from here to-night, 'twould be at peril of my life, for the hearts of the warriors are turned against me without cause."

The owl was angry at the fellow's disobedience;

but he realized that it would not be politic for him to show his anger. He was only an owl, after all, and a very small one at that. Suppose he again ordered Red Eye from the lodge, and Red Eye, for fear of the villagers, again refused to obey? He had no power of magic, as he had no power of body, to enforce the command. He would simply have to flutter, and snap his beak, and even the dull-witted Red Eye would wonder at that. No, he must be magnanimous.

" Nay, I did not mean to turn you from your lodge to-night, good friend," said the owl, in a voice that sounded like the utterance of neither man nor bird in its attempt at soft and gentle tones. " Sleep here, faithful Red Eye, here on your own couch. In the morning, after I have spoken to these hot-headed warriors, you may take up your abode in Fang's lodge and I shall inhabit that of the dead chief."

Red Eye grovelled in his gratitude, and stammered many words of thanks and praise; and at the end of it all he added, artlessly, " Never before did I hear of such a thing, great chief, of such a thing as Bright Robe's mercy."

The owl had to close his eyes, for a few seconds, fearing that the hate and rage within him might

flash visibly in those yellow orbs. Oh, for but
a shade of his old power! Oh, for but the strength
of a man, and the spirit of that blundering,
grovelling Red Eye should soon be footing the
dark trail.

" Peace," exclaimed the owl, in a voice that
trembled. " Do not put my mercy to any further
test. Go to your couch, and sleep."

Red Eye awoke at a very early hour in the morning, and began to wonder what strange dream
had possessed him in the night. Fragments of
it shook about in his poor skull.

" Something about an owl," he muttered.
" Something about a miserable little owl, and
I thought it was Bright Robe, the wicked one.
Ho, ho, what a foolish dream. And I fed it with
— with — " but his soliloquy ended in a gasping
cry. From the shadows beyond the foot of his
couch glared two yellow eyes, full upon him.

" Silence, crack-brain," snapped the owl, " and
bring me some good fresh meat. Bring me the
best in the village, fellow, or I will turn you into
a mouse and devour you."

" I thought it was a dream, great chief. I
thought it was only a dream, oh master of magicians," babbled Red Eye.

The owl ruffled his feathers, fluttered his wings, and snapped his beak; and Red Eye, taking the hint, tore open the flap that covered the doorway and fled from the lodge. He was instantly captured by two or three of his fellow-villagers, and handled none too gently.

"No more of your nonsense, Red Eye," cried one. "We've divided the goods, and set aside a share for you, and if you raise any more disturbances we'll break your empty skull."

They shook him violently, and jerked him this way and that between them, as if he were an article of value which each was eager to possess, until he bawled for mercy. At that, they redoubled their efforts.

"We heard enough from you, yesterday," they cried; and the louder he howled against their treatment the more lustily did they knock him about, informing him all the while that he was no longer of any importance in their estimation.

"My lodge! My lodge! Bright Robe is in my lodge," yelled Red Eye, at last. The voicing of this information proved a fortunate move for him.

"What do you mean, you punk-head?" cried

the tormentors, pulling and hauling at him with less vigour.

" He is there — the great magician," gasped Red Eye. " He came last night in the form of an owl."

" You've been dreaming, feather-wit," said one of the warriors, shaking him back and forth as if in hopes of curing his mental infirmities.

" Look for yourselves," groaned Red Eye. " He wants meat. He wants the best meat in the village, and raw, at that."

They released him and dashed for the lodge. They crowded and jostled one another in the entrance, each eager to have first look at whatever had put that crazy idea in Red Eye's head. Sure enough, there perched a little brown owl on a heap of Red Eye's spears. They stared, openmouthed, at the bird, amazed to find even this much of Red Eye's story to be true.

" When you have done with looking at me," said the owl, in a horrible, rusty voice, " go and get me some fresh meat."

In their efforts to escape from the baleful glare of those yellow eyes, they trod on each other's toes, tripped and sprawled and very nearly overturned the lodge. But they got away at last and dashed toward Red Eye, whom they saw approaching with a slice of raw caribou meat and a vessel of water. Strong Hunter, one of the flying group, knew that the meat must have been cut from the carcass of an animal which he had killed on the previous day; but he did not give it a thought. He halted in front of Red Eye, and the others gathered around. They were joined by a dozen more of the villagers, old Hot Tongue among them.

"What is it? Who is it?" gasped Strong Hunter. "He spoke to us — he, the little owl — and his eyes were enough to crack one's bones."

"It is as I have already told you," said Red Eye, with an assumption of dignity. "He is Bright Robe. He came to my lodge, last night, of all the fine lodges in the village. He talked with me of many things. Stand aside now, I carry food and drink to the great magician."

All except Hot Tongue were deeply impressed. Red Eye strode on, and just as he was about to enter the lodge the old woman cried after him, "There is a dead beaver, ten days dead, down by the river. Would not your master like a piece of that; he seems such a dainty feeder?"

Red Eye stepped from sight, and the warriors

and women and old men turned upon Hot Tongue and vented their wrath loudly and violently. They wanted to be heard by the inmate of the lodge, for they knew that he was a magician of some sort. No true owl ever talked the human language, or had such terrifying eyes. They shouted at Hot Tongue, calling her wicked, and rash, and many other things. And Hot Tongue's spirit was shaken, not by the anger of the people (for she knew what that was worth), but by her own words. She had seen magicians and their workings, and feared them. Cursing her foolish tongue, she turned and ran into the forest.

When the little brown owl had eaten the caribou meat, and dipped his beak into the vessel of water a few times, and cleaned the feathers of his breast, he told Red Eye to bring three of the chief men of the village into the lodge. So Red Eye went out and called for the three chief men to come to the lodge and hear the words of the great Bright Robe; and the modesty of the warriors and the old men was wonderful to behold.

Every one urged his own unimportance. By their own account, there was not a person of any consequence in the village. Strong Hunter, who had spent hours the night before in explaining his fitness for the position of chief, was now entirely of another mind; and Seven Knives, who had then been loudest of all in denying his argument, now proclaimed Strong Hunter as the perfection of manhood. Strong Hunter protested.

" I am only a poor hunter," he cried. " But you are a man of brains, Seven Knives, as you told us last night. The great Bright Robe would find wisdom in your talk."

" This is foolishness," said a woman. " Your talk is all turned backward in your mouths, for fear of the owl. Here are two old men, who have lived long enough to be of great importance, and are too weak to resist the honour. As for a third, — why, surely Red Eye is one of our chief men."

The warriors were delighted with the woman's wit, and in a moment the two poor old great-grandfathers, both deaf and more than half blind, were being pushed gently toward the owl's lodge, close on the heels of Red Eye. Every villager, — man, woman, and child — joined in the procession; but they moved cautiously, and no voice was raised save that of one of the old men. He, poor ancient, having heard nothing of his election to a belated honour, protested shrilly against the indignity of being hustled through the village.

The crowd halted at a distance of about five paces from the lodge in which the bird was waiting to hold audience. Red Eye took charge of his fellow dignitaries, at this point, and dragged them into the lodge in short order.

" What is the meaning of this? " cried the owl.

" I have done your bidding, Mighty One," stammered Red Eye. " Here are the three chief men of the village, as chosen by all the people but a minute ago."

" And you are one of the leaders of the village? " asked the owl.

" It is even so, great chief, now that you abide in my poor lodge," replied Red Eye, who had guessed the reason of his sudden rise in the estimation of the village, despite his dullness of wit, and yet was too stupid to keep it to himself.

" And why these old cripples? " asked the owl.

" Because of their exceeding age were they chosen, great chief; for it was thought that they would be wise enough to understand your wisdom, having lived so many years," replied Red Eye.

" You are too simple, Red Eye," said the owl.

"Shake your dry brain and find me another reason."

"The warriors are afraid to enter this lodge," cried Red Eye, delighted at his penetration into the matter. "Yes, great chief, they are afraid, for they know that they deserve no mercy. Only the innocent are without fear."

"You have a wonderful mind. I shall certainly make you chief of this village," said the owl. "Now you may let these old cripples depart," he added.

Red Eye pushed the old men from the lodge; and off they hobbled, muttering angrily. They had not seen the owl, because of their blindness, and they had not heard his voice, because of their deafness; so they were still at a loss to know what all the trouble was about.

"Now tell me the names of some of the most cunning and strong warriors in this village," said the owl.

"Seven Knives is a powerful man," replied Red Eye. "And so is Strong Hunter. Yellow Fox is also loud at the council fire, and Mighty Hand thinks himself as great as any."

"Yes," said the owl. "I know them all. I have watched them, even when they thought me a thousand miles away. They are not as great as they appear to be; and they will be even of less importance before many days. But, for a little while, we must let them think they are deserving of honour, so that we may read every design in their hearts."

Red Eye was deeply impressed.

"I am your servant, mighty magician," he replied. "I live but to obey your commands."

"'Tis well," said the owl. "Go cautiously, and repeat nothing of what I say to you in private concerning the greatness to which I intend to raise you so soon. Now order Strong Hunter to come to me, alone. I would read his very soul."

Red Eye backed from the lodge, and found the people clustered outside, eagerly waiting for him. He approached them, and pointed a finger at Strong Hunter.

"The mighty Bright Robe has sent for you," he said.

CHAPTER XVIII

THE MAKER OF CHIEFS

WHEN Strong Hunter, after a lengthy stay within the lodge, appeared again among his fellows, he looked both elated and impressed and would answer none of their questions. But he told them that the little brown owl was Bright Robe, without a doubt; also, that no chief would be appointed for the village until the end of two moons' time, and that the magician himself would act as their chief until then. There was some grumbling at that, among the warriors, but no open objection. The owl had told Strong Hunter the same story that he had told Red Eye, and had made him the same promises of reward. Also, he had not forgotten to charge him to keep those promises secret.

He had made a great deal of fun of poor Red Eye to the hunter. And he had told him to have a huge fire built that night, and to tell the villagers the story of his fight with Wise-as-a-she-wolf and of his victory.

When night fell, a heap of wood as high as a
lodge was lit in a dozen places, and the whole
village clustered around it. The men wore battle-
feathers in their hair and carried their spears and
war-clubs, for Strong Hunter had promised them
that it was to be a great occasion. As Strong
Hunter began the story of the great battle between the magicians, the owl's version of it, Red
Eye took his seat quietly among the warriors, and
looked at the orator with a covert and supercilious
smile. He had but just come from the owl's
lodge; and the owl had explained to him, in the
most friendly manner, that the seeming considera-
tion with which he had treated Strong Hunter
was but a sly step toward that warrior's undoing.
He had looked so wise, and sly, and friendly, that
Red Eye had felt quite satisfied.

"We will play with the vain fellows, for the
space of two moons," the owl had concluded.

Strong Hunter stood upright and waved his
arms above his head, shaking a spear in one hand
and a club in the other.

" This is the story of the battle between two
magicians," he cried, " between Bright Robe,
the master of magic, and Wise-as-a-she-wolf, the
child of vanity."

He pranced forward a few steps, and back again, and twirled about on his toes. The black battle-feathers flashed in his long braid of tow-coloured hair. These islanders were not red men, like the inhabitants of the great lands to the south and west.

" Before Bright Robe could strike a blow," he continued, " the other turned and fled, speeding like a flying brant, for the moccasins of the wind were on his feet. But Bright Robe sprang after him through the air, reached him and hurled him to earth. Unable to escape, Wise-as-a-she-wolf fought with all his strength and cunning; and Bright Robe returned him two blows for every one received."

Here Strong Hunter swung his club, smiting an imaginary foe, and thrust with his spear so violently that his audience shrank away from him. He skipped and pranced, struck desperate attitudes, and shouted like a madman.

" Blood flies," he continued. " Trees bend, and crash to the ground. The hills shake and great rocks roll into the valleys. The strength of Wise-as-a-she-wolf dwindles and his courage runs out with his blood. He strikes wide. He strikes feebly. But Bright Robe feels no weariness.

His blows redouble their speed and weight. He beats his enemy to the ground. He bends, takes the limp body in his hands, and hurls it over the mountain-top."

Ceasing the narrative suddenly, Strong Hunter once more put his body and limbs in motion. He staggered, and reeled, in the person of Wise-as-a-she-wolf. He sprang high in air, and delivered heroic strokes, in the person of Bright Robe. At last he stooped to the earth, set his hands on an imaginary body and hurled it far over the heads of the enraptured villagers. Then, drawing himself to his full height, he folded his arms on his breast and stood silent and motionless.

The applause was quick and loud. Even Seven Knives and Red Eye joined in it. Old men, who had long since forgotten their days of prowess, flung their arms about as if in desperate conflict. Young men sprang from their seats and danced around the fire, brandishing their weapons. The graver warriors shouted, and beat their clubs on the ground. All were affected by the orator's efforts as if they had drunk deeply of the strong wine of crushed and fermented berries.

Elated by his success, Strong Hunter went straight to the owl's lodge. The bird received

him with gracious words, for the roars of applause
had reached his ears.

"You have done well," he said. "I see that
you are already powerful among the people, that
my good-will toward you is already giving you
new power. This will be the greatest village in
the land, when you are its chief. Go now, Strong
Hunter, and send my servant Red Eye to
me."

Strong Hunter bowed, and left the lodge. He
found Red Eye still seated by the fire, smiling a
twisted, evil smile. Without ceremony, he
ordered him to go to the magician. Red Eye
glanced up at him, with a glow under his lids.

"Go to your master," said Strong Hunter
again, and still more roughly. Red Eye went,
without a word; but there was rage in his heart.
He wondered what had passed in the lodge, to so
soon change the warrior's manner with him. He
vowed that Strong Hunter should be the first to
feel his wrath, when the village was in his power.
He felt a dim distrust of the magician.

The little brown owl read what was in Red
Eye's mind.

"Strong Hunter is a conceited fellow," he said.
"His vanity amuses me."

" It does not amuse me, great chief," replied
Red Eye.

" You are of too serious a nature, my friend,"
said the owl. " But I think the bursting of that
rascal's vanity will amuse even you."

" Oh, mightily," cried the other. " I would
give ten hides to see him brought low this very
night. I would gladly give a beaver skin for
every cry of pain he would utter if I could but
stick my knife into his big body."

" Have patience," said the owl. " It is my
pleasure to sit inactive for a little while, and study
the natures of these people, their hopes and
vanities and foolish affairs. When I am tired of
it, then 'twill be time enough for you to break
the pride, yea, even the neck, of Strong
Hunter."

Red Eye went away from the lodge and medi-
tated. Though he was a coward, he had none of
that fear which is a foretaste of remorse. Let
him but get an enemy in his power, with no chance
to strike back, and he would show no mercy.
Pity was a sensation unknown to him; and if he
sometimes appeared to speak honestly, it was
entirely due to his dulness of wit. Now he retired to an empty lodge and gave his poor mind

to this matter of Strong Hunter's arrogance of
manner. Why had Strong Hunter been chosen
to tell the story of the battle to the villagers?
Why had Strong Hunter walked so proudly from
the owl's lodge? He thought and thought and
thought, until his head felt as if it would fly into
a dozen fragments, so great was the effort of
concentration. He saw a glimmer of the truth;
but no, all was darkness again.

Sometime during the next day, the owl managed to have a secret talk with Seven Knives;
and to him he told the same tales, and made the
same promises, as to Strong Hunter and Red
Eye. Also, he charged him to secrecy.

Three days passed without incident; but on
the morning of the fourth day Red Eye lay with
an ear at the edge of the lodge while Strong
Hunter and the owl talked within. He crawled
away, before Strong Hunter left the lodge. An
hour later, he sprang upon the big warrior, from
behind, struck a blow and shouted the treachery
of the owl. The blow glanced from the great
muscles of Strong Hunter's neck, but sent him
reeling, for all that. Then Red Eye turned to
flee, still shouting of the owl's treachery. The
wounded man staggered after him and hurled his

stone axe, blindly but with terrific force. It struck Red Eye on the back of the skull.

In a second, the whole village was in an uproar. Red Eye lay dead on the ground; but his last words were alive in men's ears. Seven Knives stood face to face with Strong Hunter and asked if there was truth in what Red Eye had shouted.

" 'Tis true that the owl has promised that I am to be chief of this village," replied Strong Hunter.

" He promised the same to me," said Seven Knives.

" And there is another chief," said Yellow Fox, pointing at the body of Red Eye.

" I think if that little owl were really Bright Robe, he would have shown himself in his true form before this," said Old Hot Tongue. " Bright Robe would have killed me, for what I said about the beaver meat," she added.

" He is Bright Robe, and none other. He knows things that only Bright Robe or Wise-as-a-she-wolf could know," said Strong Hunter.

" Then why does he sit in the lodge all day, and eat raw flesh? " asked an old man. " Bright Robe never lets a day pass without some violence or theft."

" He is Bright Robe, for all that," said Seven Knives. " And I think he is still as wicked as he ever was."

" I once beheld the eyes of the devil that lives deep in the salt water," said Strong Hunter, " and though they were green and big, they were not more wicked than the eyes of that little owl."

" I do not fear any bird that flies," said a young man, and before they could lay hands upon him, he was running swiftly toward the lodge in which sat the owl.

" I have a good bow here, and a sharp arrow," he cried, as he ran.

At that the owl shot from the lodge and flew swiftly away across the river.

" There goes your mighty magician, your maker of chiefs," said the young man.

The villagers stared in wonder after the departing bird, and continued to stand and stare long after it had vanished.

A few hours after the owl's hurried departure, a party of men who belonged farther up the river arrived at the village. They were on their way to the southern coast of the island, to kill the seals that came down on the ice through the Narrow Sea. When they had heard the story of the owl, one of them told of how he had been sick early in the spring, and had gone to the lodge of Old Whispering Grass, the doctor, far inland near the great lake. And he told them of the fight between the magicians, as the old woman had told it to him; of Bright Robe's defeat and of the spell upon him which would keep him in the shape of a little owl until five summers were gone.

The people of the village were amazed and disgusted at the memory of the fear in which they had stood of the harmless bird. "But Bright Robe never forgets an injury," said one of the old men, "and I hope that I may have died peacefully before those five seasons are passed."

CHAPTER XIX

THE THEFT OF THE RED FEATHERS

ALL went well with the baby in the good magician's lodge. He remembered nothing of the world and the people that were without the magic walls; and yet, when Run-all-day visited him, he knew him and ran to him. His days were full of quiet play and happy, childish fancies. The wonderful pictures on the walls were his playmates; and he learned their meanings, gradually but without effort. He felt no loneliness or fear, even when Wise-as-a-she-wolf was away from the lodge. But he was seldom alone, for the magician was so happy in the company of his adopted baby that he forgot many of his great affairs in the world. He would lie awake all night, planning games, wonderful, magic games, to play with the little fellow next day. And he painted some more pictures on the walls, thus expanding the great lesson-book. He painted the flight of Jumping Wolf through the wilderness, and the young warrior's rescue from the ice, all in the magic pigments that made them true as real earth and real water and clear as sunlight. So the baby, toddling from picture to picture, absorbed knowledge of men and beasts, of battles and the chase, of gentleness and honesty, and of the ugliness of evil.

In August, a stranger arrived at Run-all-day's village and asked to be allowed to remain and become a member of the new clan. He was of darker complexion than was usual among the islanders and his hair was black and straight. He gave his name as Spotted Seal. He said that he had been born far in the west, close to the shore of the Narrow Sea, and had been a lonely warrior all his life. Run-all-day did not accept him at once, but allowed him to fish and hunt with the villagers, so that he might prove himself a safe and worthy man. Spotted Seal soon won the respect of the clansmen, in spite of his black, shifting eyes; for he was a good worker and a strong man with all manner of weapons. He was a cunning and tireless hunter, and skilled in the management of canoes.

Spotted Seal had not been an inmate of the village many days, when he heard some gossip

of the red feathers, from old Green Bow. He
showed no interest in the subject, indifferently
mending a fishing-line while Green Bow told of
the wonderful power of the feathers; of how he
had seen the chief slip them into his moccasins;
of how it was rumoured that Red Willow took
care of them and kept them in a leathern bag,
along with other of her precious possessions.
Spotted Seal looked indifferent, all the while
the old man talked, but his heart was thumping
madly. He had a slight knowledge of magic,
and a great desire to enlarge that knowledge.
He was ambitious of power; and this talk of the
magic feathers, which carried a man through the
air like the wings of a hawk, filled him with a
fever of covetousness. But he did not show his
emotions by so much as the flicker of an eyelash;
and yet it was for this very thing that he had
come to the village. He had heard something of
Run-all-day's power of flight, in a vague, round-
about way, and so had travelled many days to
investigate the secret of the matter. He had
never heard of the chief of the distant village as
a magician, and he could not believe that he was
possessed of the famous moccasins of the wind.
Now he was glad to hear that the wonder lay in

two small feathers and not in the chief's own person, for it would be an easier matter to steal feathers from a man than wisdom out of his brain.

So Spotted Seal began to spy on the chief's lodge, creeping and peering about at all hours of the night. At last he was rewarded for his exertions by seeing Red Willow take the feathers from the bag, smooth them tenderly between her fingers, and return them to their hiding-place. Then he saw her place the bag under the skins on Run-all-day's couch. His eager glance took note of the exact spot where she hid the bag. It was a small bag, of white leather, decorated with designs worked in dyed porcupine quills. As the night was still young, he stole away and joined some other men at the fire, and calmly listened to their stories and took part in their talk.

In that darkest hour before the first glimmer of dawn, Spotted Seal crawled to the closed entrance of the chief's lodge, and lay, for nearly a minute, with his ear at the bottom of the great flap of hide. He heard no sound from within, save the gentle and regular breathing of the sleepers. He raised the flap a little, very cau-

tiously, and thrust his head under it. Inch by
inch, and without the slightest sound, he wormed
himself beneath the edge of the hide and into the
lodge. Then again he lay still for some time,
listening, straining his eyes against the blackness,
and drawing his breath guardedly. Again he
advanced, crawling almost flat, with one hand held
in front of him so lightly that, should it touch a
sleeper, it would give no shock of contact. At
last he felt that he was beside the couch on which
lay the chief. He could hear that warrior's
breath, close in his ears, and he trembled. Now
his hand touched the furs, and slipped beneath
them and encountered the precious bag that
contained the red feathers. At that, his heart
thumped so heavily that it deafened his ears
against the sound of the chief's breathing. For
what seemed a long time to him, he crouched,
motionless, beside the couch, with one hand on
the bag of leather. But at last he gathered courage
to draw it forth. He heard the chief stir uneasily
then lie quiet again. Some one, evidently a
child, whimpered in its dreams. He turned and
crawled back toward the entrance of the lodge
lifted the flap of hide again and wriggled under it
and out to the wider blackness of the open

After moving away from the lodge for a short distance, he seated himself on a boulder, opened the bag and thrust his hand within. He soon discovered the red feathers among needles of bone, trinkets of shell and jasper, and other such trifles. He placed one in the sole of each of his moccasins, and tied them securely to his feet.

Spotted Seal stood up and looked about him. The sky, the forests, and the earth at his feet, were all massed in a vast blackness. A little stirring of wind, but newly arisen, moved around him. He shivered, though the air was mild. Thought of the potent magic against the soles of his feet, and of the terrific flight which he had the power to take, up and across the blackness, shook his heart and unstrung his muscles. For a moment he wished that he had not taken the feathers, and even thought of returning them to the chief's lodge. But no, he would not again face the danger of entering that lodge and crawling about so near to that strong warrior. And the feathers were a great prize, surely one of the greatest possessions in the world. And now they were his.

" I am a coward," he whispered, huskily. " I have run the risk of my life in stealing the feathers from the chief's couch, from under his body; and now I have not the courage to use them. It is so dark; but when daylight comes I shall fly into the air like a bird."

But he knew that it would not be safe for him to wait, so near the village, for morning. The chief might awake at any moment and discover the absence of the precious feathers; and if that should happen — well, Spotted Seal had been long enough in Run-all-day's village to learn to fear that big warrior's displeasure. So he turned his face from the quiet lodges and set out through the darkness. After having travelled for more than a mile, he halted suddenly and uttered an exclamation of disgust. He had come away from the village with no weapons except the short flint knife in his belt. The great undertaking of stealing the bag from the chief's lodge had driven all thought of bow, spear, and arrows from his mind. The day was breaking now, in a clear, colourless streak along the east. Would he return to the village, and to his own lodge, and arm himself? The people would still be asleep, and the magic feathers were on his feet. Yes, he would go back, for he had left many trusty weapons in his lodge, and fish-hooks of bone, and some good fish-lines. Even if a man can fly like a bird, he reflected, still he must hunt and fish, if he would live.

So Spotted Seal turned back toward the village, from which he had stolen so fearfully but a little while before. The light of day increased swiftly, flooding the eastern sky with crimson and bright gold. Spotted Seal quickened his pace, afraid that the village might be astir by the time he should reach it. Soon he was able to see the lodges in front, between the ranks of the forests, the sunlight gleaming on their peaks. Now he advanced more cautiously, and was about to issue from the trees when a loud cry caused him to halt and crouch like a startled animal.

The cry was from the lips of Run-all-day, who had discovered that the bag in which the magic feathers were kept was gone from beneath the skins on his couch. Next moment, he ran from his lodge, and shouted for the men of the village, old and young, to gather in all haste. They were before him within the minute, wondering but ready. He glanced over them quickly.

"Where is Spotted Seal?" he asked. "Go to his lodge and find him."

The warriors rushed to the lodge of the stranger,

tore it open, and shouted that it was empty; and
at the same moment Spotted Seal turned from his
contemplation of the scene and started to run.
But he had forgotten the feathers in his moccasins.
The first stride lifted him from the ground and
dashed him among the tree-tops. He uttered a
loud scream of amazement and fear, which was
answered angrily from the village. The voices
of the warriors, lifted in fierce and eager hunting-
cries, steadied his wits. He sprang clear of the
trees and soared away to the southward. The
people of Run-all-day's village beheld him thus
mount into their view and then fly swiftly beyond
it; and they sent a howl of rage and a few harmless arrows after him.

Spotted Seal felt like a man in the clutches of
an awful dream, during the first few minutes of
his flight. The world — river, forest, and hill —
sped backward beneath him with sickening
velocity. The air sang in his ears, and his breath
seemed beaten back against mouth and nostrils.
The glory of the morning and the rushing air
upon his eyeballs, almost blinded him, and the
fear of falling to earth was so strong in him that he
continued, for some time, to exert every muscle,
like a runner in a race.

But, in time, he slackened his pace, for very weariness, and then he found that he could continue in the air with but little effort and no discomfort. He scarcely moved his feet, and yet sailed pleasantly and safely above the forests. His eyes cleared and his breath came back to him. He swooped gently toward the earth and swerved easily up again, finding this matter of flight to be as pleasant as it was amazing. He circled high; he flew this way and that; he ran across the tops of the forest trees, just touching them with his feet. But he continued to increase the distance between himself and the village.

It was not until noon that Spotted Seal felt the gnawings of hunger, and realized that the knife in his belt was the only weapon in his possession. But now he felt no fear of starving, and cared no more for the loss of his bow and arrow than if meat was to be picked from the ground, like berries. He would hunt as hawks hunt, with the advantage that no cover of brush or branches could cheat him of his quarry. So he flew low, and kept a sharp watch. A covey of grouse flew up from a barren and lit in a thicket of small spruces. He swooped down and beat the tops of the trees with a short stick, hovering above them all the while. Out flew the grouse, in all directions; and in a moment one had received a sharp blow from the stick and lay dead on the ground. Another was soon killed by the same means. Then Spotted Seal chose a nook that suited him, lit a fire, and set to work to cook his belated breakfast.

CHAPTER XX

A JOURNEY TO THE MAGIC FOREST

RUN - ALL - DAY was very much ashamed, and very angry, at the loss of the magic feathers which the good Wise-as-a-she-wolf had trusted to his care. So hot was his anger at first, that it clouded his wits, and he set out in pursuit of the thief and ran for fully six miles before he realized that he might just as well chase a hawk as Spotted Seal. When that thought came to him, he immediately leaned against a tree, to recover his breath and plan some other means of regaining possession of the red feathers. He had not filled his lungs more than a dozen times before Jumping Wolf, who had followed close on his heels, halted before him. The chief eyed the youth mournfully.

" We are mighty runners, lad," he said, " but only the moccasins of the wind can overtake the feet that are shod with the red feathers."

" He flew southward," replied Jumping Wolf,

" and if I follow, day and night, I may come upon him while he sleeps, or see him in the air and bring him down with an arrow. All I need is a wallet of pemmican and a quiver of arrows, and then I am ready for the journey. I have hit hawks and eagles while they flew above the tree-tops, so surely I can put an arrow into Spotted Seal."

The chief shook his head dejectedly.

" Let us go home. I must ask Red Willow what is to be done," he said.

So the two swift runners returned to the village, meeting the other warriors breathless and still staggering forward, scattered along the way. So. they returned to the lodge, together, all depressed by the loss of the feathers and ill tempered from having run so far on empty stomachs.

The chief went straight to Red Willow, and confessed to her that he could think of no way of recovering the precious feathers.

" Wise-as-a-she-wolf must be told about it," said she, after a moment's reflection. " He will be able to get them back again; and I do not think he will be angry with us when he knows how Spotted Seal crept into our lodge, in the night-time, and stole them."

" But even if he is not angry, he will not trust me with the feathers again," said the chief.

" 'Twill be better so, I believe," replied the woman, " for now that people know about them, and of the great virtue they possess, they will be a dangerous possession for any man save a magician."

" But how am I to tell him about it? " asked Run-all-day. " 'Tis a long journey to his lodge, and even when the journey is made a man cannot see the lodge until the master charms his eyes. This is the truth, for he told us so. And I cannot leave the village, for the warriors would soon begin to argue about this and that, and all my good work would be blown away as the ashes of a dead fire are scattered by the wind."

" And still must the good magician be told the whole story, or his enemies may use the feathers against him while he thinks them safe in your keeping," said Red Willow.

At that moment Jumping Wolf looked in at the door of the lodge.

" Here is a messenger for you to send," said Red Willow. " He is swift and strong, and worthy of trust. Come in," she added, to the young man, " and hear what the chief has to ask you."

Jumping Wolf entered immediately and looked at Run-all-day with eager inquiry in his glance.

" Will you go a long journey for me? " asked the chief. " I think it is a three days' journey, for one who walks, from here to the lodge of Wise-as-a-she-wolf."

" Tell me the road and I will go," replied the young man.

So the chief told him the way, as well as he could from the memory of what he had seen in his flights. He told him that the magician's lodge lay to the westward, beyond two large rivers and many streams, a great barren and many wooded hills. He told him of the pine wood and the high mountains, and how he must search the pine wood for a little pond and then shout that he had a message for Wise-as-a-she-wolf from Run-all-day.

" And the message? " asked Jumping Wolf.

" Tell him that the red feathers have been stolen from my lodge, and describe to him the face and figure of the thief," replied Run-all-day.

" And beg him to tell you of my baby. Even ask him to let you see him," said the woman.

After supplying himself with a small bag of food, and arming himself with a knife, a bow and a dozen of his best arrows, Jumping Wolf set out on his long journey. He was proud that he, a man from the south, had been chosen, from all the warriors of the village, for the task of finding the magic lodge and giving the chief's message. He had no fear of the hardships of the journey, for he loved adventure as duller men love soft couches and the warmth of the cooking-fire. So swiftly did he travel that he came to the shore of the first of the big rivers that lay in his path at just about the time of sunset. Heavy forests clothed both banks of the stream, which was fully a mile in width. He could see no smoke of fires, or any sign of human life, in any direction. After eating a little of the pemmican from his bag, he made a couch of spruce branches and lay down to sleep, without building a fire.

Jumping Wolf slept soundly until midnight, when he was awakened by the noise of something moving close beside him. He did not spring to his feet, or even sit up; but he put his hand on his knife and waited, with every sense on the alert. Again he heard the sounds that had awakened him, and he knew that a bear was close by but moving slowly away. He strained his eyes in the dim starlight, and managed, at last, to detect the vague shape of the animal against the surrounding shadows. Well, a bear was nothing to be afraid of. Now it had ceased to move; but by the sounds it made it was evidently engaged in devouring something, with ponderous relish.

" I wonder what the black glutton has found? " muttered Jumping Wolf, at the same time feeling about, with his right hand, in the moss beside his couch. On finding a good-sized stone, he threw it at the disturber of his slumbers. It was well aimed; and the bear uttered a protesting grunt and shambled into the woods. The young man listened to the sounds of the beast's retreat until they faded away in the distance; then he closed his eyes and returned to his slumbers.

When Jumping Wolf opened his eyes again, with the first flush of morning light, he discovered that the bag of pemmican was gone from where he had placed it close beside his couch, the evening before. Then he remembered the visit of the bear, and sprang to his feet, and ran to where he had seen the animal during the night. There lay the bag, ripped open and empty; but a few scraps of the pemmican remained, scattered about on the ground. At first the young man was angry and somewhat dismayed. But presently he laughed aloud.

" If I had known what you were eating, old glutton," he said, " I would have disturbed your meal with an arrow instead of with a harmless little stone. But I am glad to see that you were so polite as to leave me enough for my breakfast."

And with that he stooped down, gathered the fragments of pemmican in his hands, and ate them with relish; after which he slaked his thirst at a little spring which trickled from the mossy rocks close beside him. Then he fastened his bow and quiver of arrows securely together, tied them high across his shoulders, and stepped down the shore and into the river. The water felt chilly at first; but the sun was shining brightly and the mists were quickly dispersing from the wide current. He waded in, deeper and deeper at every stride, and when the water was half-way up his breast he leaned forward and struck out with hands and feet. The strokes of his swimming were long, slow, and powerful, propelling him easily and steadily across the current. Now his blood was in a glow, for he was strong and young.

The surface of the river was bright as gold with the level rays of the sun, and the swimmer rejoiced in the freshness and glory of the morning. Sometimes he lowered his head so that the bright refreshing water might wash over it.

When Jumping Wolf landed on the farther shore, he felt no fatigue from his long swim, but began immediately to leap about, and swing his arms, so as to shake some of the weight of water from his leather clothing. He unfastened his bow and arrows from his shoulders, returned the quiver to the left side of his girdle, and replaced the wet bow-string with a dry one from a watertight wallet which was attached to his belt. The restringing of the bow was no more than completed when he heard the whistle of wings, and on looking up saw three ducks hurtling toward him with outstretched necks. They saw him, and swerved to one side; but the bow-string twanged, an arrow swished in the air, and one of the ducks quacked loudly and fell into the shallow water at the edge of the river.

"Here is my dinner; and it is better than musty pemmican," said the young man, as he drew forth the arrow and fastened the dead bird to his belt. Then, very well satisfied with himself, and the

world in general, he continued on the second stage
of his westward journey.

Jumping Wolf travelled steadily until noon,
then lit a fire by means of friction — a laborious
method of grinding one stick into another — and
broiled the fat duck. He was now at the edge of
a great barren, a vast plain of rocky hummocks,
mellow, berry-swarded levels and occasional
clumps of stunted spruces.

The season of the wild harvest was over the
land, the days of ripe berries and falling seeds,
and the flocking birds. Snipe and plover from
the farther north, and coveys of ptarmigan, and
flocks of snow birds, fed along the ground and
started up on quick wings, on every side. The
sun, wheeling high in the blue, touched that wide,
treeless place with a mellow enchantment that
stole into the heart of Jumping Wolf with pleasant
languor — a suggestion of idleness and dreams.
The berry-starred moss on which he reclined was
warm as a couch of fox skins, and the soft bird-
calls, sounding indolently from hummock and
hollow, made music in his ears. A sweet, elusive
fragrance, that was the breath of the warmth and
ripeness of the barren, stole into his brain. Millions of red berries, millions of little, tinted leaves,

innumerable pockets of warm, brown loam, loosed that fragrance on the air at the soft entreaty of the sun. And the warmth of the sun penetrated also to the very bones of the young hunter, until he lay at full length on the moss and sighed with the comfort of it. His eyelids fluttered down. He had travelled far and swiftly, and crossed a river full of chilly water; then why should he not lie here for a little while, basking in the sun, and dream a little of Singing Bird, the daughter of the chief?

The temptation to rest and dream was strong; but not strong enough to deaden for long Jumping Wolf's sense of duty. Had not his benefactor, Run-all-day, trusted him to carry an important message with all speed? Then how could he throw away good hours of daylight in idle dreaming? So he forced himself to arise from the warm moss and harden his heart against the drowsiness of the noon.

By nightfall the youth had reached the western margin of the barren, and made his resting-place for the night beside a brook that ran through groves of pines and spruces. He had killed two grouse on the way, and had halted several times to refresh himself with handfuls of the tart,

juicy partridge berries. Again he gathered little
fragments of wood, dry as tinder, laboriously
created the speck of red flame and enlarged it to a
cooking-fire. He cooked both the birds, so that
he would not lose time in the morning in preparing
his breakfast.

Jumping Wolf reached the great forest of pine,
in which stood the lodge of Wise-as-a-she-wolf,
early in the afternoon of the third day of his
journey. He climbed a high tree at the edge of
the wood, and from its top looked far and wide
on all sides, studying the features of the land-
scape. After a short survey he felt satisfied that
this was the place which the chief had described
to him; so, without further hesitation, he descended to the ground and struck into the wood
in search of the pond of crystal water.

The sun had dipped below the tree-tops, and the
western sky was red as fire, when Jumping Wolf
issued from the ranks of straight pine boles and
halted on the margin of the little lake. The oval
surface of water was red with the reflection of the
sky, and lay there like a warrior's shield of painted
hide. On every side towered the pines, ancient, gigantic, brooding above the secrets of their still
hearts. They were robed in dusk, and their wide

branches were heavy with massed shadows; but their tops were aflame with the light of the hidden sun. Jumping Wolf breathed softly. He could hear nothing; there was no sound in all that enchanted forest save the beating of his own heart. The red faded from the sky and slipped from the spires of the trees. The lake shone duskily, lost its glow, clouded and lay like dead ice.

Then the spirit of Jumping Wolf shook itself from the spell that had stolen about it. He raised his head and shouted the name of the great magician. The echoes rang quickly back to him, just beyond the narrow water, in among the pines. The name he had cried clanged about him, clanged and leaped, shattering the brooding silence of the place with a note of menace, then dropped to silence again. The young man's heart was shaken. He glanced backward, over his shoulder, and his muscles grew tense, as if for a great effort. But what had he to fear in the wood of the kind magician? His courage returned at that thought, and again he lifted his voice.

" I am Jumping Wolf," he cried, " and I bring word from Run-all-day."

His voice rang clear across the little water. But he drew back, as if threatened by a blow, when the silence closed instantly over the words he had shouted so bravely. There was no echo. The sound of his voice had rung high, and fallen dead. And yet the place had clashed with echo at his first cry. He trembled with a horror of something vague, gigantic, imminent. He would have turned and fled, dashed blindly away from this power that loosed and choked the echoes at its will, but he had no strength to lift his feet from the ground.

A voice spoke to him, by name, from the other side of the dark pond. It was the voice of the good magician, calm and gentle, as he remembered having heard it in the village of Run-all-day.

" Have no fear, Jumping Wolf. My friends are safe in this forest. Bring me the message," said the voice.

The young man fought down the terror that still shook him, and with a great effort of will forced his craven feet to the master's bidding.

CHAPTER XXI

THE QUEST OF THE FEATHERS

JUMPING WOLF stumbled around the margin of the lake, felt the touch of a guiding hand on his arm, and saw, suddenly, the glowing windows of the magic lodge. Next moment, as the thing would happen in a dream, he stood within the bright room, staring at the living pictures on the walls and the lamps that burned so steadily and yet exhaled no smoke. He uttered an exclamation of wonder, happiness. Surely he had entered the lodge of the gods! Then he felt a light touch against his knee, and looking down beheld Run-all-day's littlest baby smiling up at him.

"What is the message, friend, that you bring from the honest Run-all-day?" inquired the magician, who stood close at his elbow.

"I had forgotten it," whispered the youth. "It seems a small matter, a thing to snap one's fingers over, in this beautiful place," and straightway his eyes began to wander along the walls again and up at the starlit roof.

" You have come a long journey," said Wise-as-a-she-wolf, gently.

The young man sighed and withdrew his gaze from the picture of a battle.

" The red feathers are gone from the chief's lodge, O mighty one," he said. " They were stolen in the night, from the robes of the chief's couch, by a stranger named Spotted Seal. We gave chase to the thief, for a matter of several miles, but he flew like a hawk. And Run-all-day could not leave the village, so he trusted me to bring you the word, mighty chief."

The magician looked thoughtful, but not greatly disturbed. With Bright Robe reduced to harm-lessness, he did not foresee any serious difficulty in recovering possession of the feathers.

" In which direction did Spotted Seal fly? " he asked.

" He started southward, master," replied the youth.

" It is well that you arrived to-night," said the magician, " for I intended to set out on a journey early in the morning."

Jumping Wolf thought of how nearly he had given himself to slumber one noontime, and of how a few hours' rest then would have delayed him so that he would not have reached the pine wood until after the magician's departure, and so would not have found the magic lodge at all. But he said nothing of this.

" You go on a journey? Then what of the child? " he said.

" He will be safe and happy," replied Wise-as-a-she-wolf. " Everything that he may require is at his hand, and he will not know that I am gone from him. But he will know well when I return, and will be glad of it."

" I can believe that readily, great chief, for I myself could spend an hundred years in the contemplation of these wonderful pictures," replied the young man.

" And yet," said the other, thoughtfully, " this lodge was never so wonderful to me as it has become since I brought the baby to it. Now I find it hard to cross the threshold and go about my business in the world."

But this was all lost upon Jumping Wolf, who was again intent on the contemplation of the pictures of life. There was a girl that reminded him of Singing Bird; and at last he caught sight of the newest picture, and beheld, with pride and wonder, himself on the sodden ice-cake, and the big canoe paddled by Run-all-day, and Singing Bird in the bow, slim and glowing as in her living flesh. Before that picture he stood fascinated, forgetful of the magician and his surroundings.

" Nowhere in the whole world is there such another as little Singing Bird," he cried, very low, but with a quaver in his voice.

" And nowhere, north, east, south, or west, is there so great a magician as Youth," said Wise-as-a-she-wolf, smiling somewhat pathetically.

The other looked at him swiftly; and though he did not understand, he felt a vague stirring of pity for the mighty one.

Early in the morning, the magician guided Jumping Wolf out of the forest of pines and faced him on his way. He gave him a store of food to last him three days.

" Tell the mother that all is well with the littlest warrior," he said, " and say to the chief that I do not hold the loss of the feathers against him; but that, with the knowledge of them abroad among the people, I must keep them myself should I win them back, until such time as the child is ready to use them. Be guarded in your talk about this lodge of mine, and the way to it," he added.

" May I not speak of its wonders to any one? " asked the young man.

" You need not sit with a silent tongue before the maid," replied Wise-as-a-she-wolf. " I have been young, also," he added, and turned upon the other a face as boyish as the warrior's own.

Then they parted, one going southward and one eastward, and the silence of the wilderness fell again upon wood and barren. The magician walked like any common traveller, for a mile or more, pondering deeply. His thoughts were not of the red feathers, but of the little child playing by itself in the magic house. " Wonderful! Wonderful! " he murmured. " How he grows, day by day. And he loves me. My eyes require no magic keenness to see that he loves me." He sat down on a mossy stone, and his mind was not on his affairs as the guardian of a nation. He thought of the child whom he had taken into his care; and he thought how happy a man might be, a chief of a little village, or even a fisher of cod, with a woman and children in his lodge. " I must not lead him too far in the knowledge of hidden things," he reflected, " or else, in his power, he will miss the happiness that is his birthright."

At last he got to his feet. " I must find those

red feathers," he said. " I must hasten in the search of Spotted Seal; and perhaps I can return to the littlest warrior before night."

Then he hid himself in his magic and sprang into the air on the moccasins of the wind.

Wise-as-a-she-wolf flew fast and far, scanning the woods and hills and open places beneath his feet. He flashed, invisible, southward, eastward, and westward, and descended into many camps and villages, to look closely at their unsuspecting inhabitants. But nowhere did he find a man answering to Jumping Wolf's description of Spotted Seal. Just before the time of sunset, he turned his face toward home, and flew with more eagerness than he had as yet exhibited during the day. He would continue his search for Spotted Seal in the morning; but now it was time for him to tell the story of one or other of the pictures to the littlest warrior. He felt no great anxiety concerning the feathers. He was sure to find them in a day or two, before the thief could accomplish much harm with them, even if he were so minded.

Wise-as-a-she-wolf spent the next day in a fruitless search for the red feathers. He sought far and wide, and made inquiries for Spotted Seal

at several widely separated villages; but all this
without any success. It was not until the fifth
day of his search that an old fisherman, who lived
on the coast of the Narrow Sea, told of how days
before, he had been amazed to see a man running
in the air, high above the salt water, running
westward toward the hazy line of that distant
shore.

The magician crossed the water without delay,
flying unseen from under the very eyes of the
astonished fisherman. He descended to the
ground and took on his visible form, near the
camp of a party of Mountain People. He walked
into the camp, a modest, undersized youth, and
in a second a dozen great wolf-dogs had sprung
toward him, followed by several warriors. The
dogs were huge beasts, more savage and fearless
than their brothers, the timber wolves, and as
strong of jaw and limb. But under the mild
regard of the stranger's clear eyes, they halted
in their rush, turned and slunk away. The warriors were also savage in appearance, and long of
limb and hair. They were dark of skin, and black
of eye, like Spotted Seal. The truth is, Spotted
Seal had the blood of these Mountain People
strong in his veins; but how this thing had come

about is apart from our story. The warriors, more courageous than the dogs, continued their advance upon the helpless-looking stranger.

" I would speak with Black Eagle," said the magician, for these people were well known to him. At that they halted, eyeing him distrustfully.

" Black Eagle is our chief," said one, an angular fellow, with sinister eyes, a scar on his chin, and a spear in his hand. He seemed to be watching, hungrily, for something to serve as an excuse for an attack on the visitor.

" Yes, he is your chief. I want to speak with him," said the stranger, quietly.

" He is a mighty chief," said the fellow with the scar on his chin. " He does not come to every one's bidding. I will call an old woman to take your message."

" Tell him that Wise-as-a-she-wolf is waiting to talk to him," said the magician.

At that name the warriors were visibly disturbed, and several of them slunk away in much the same manner as the dogs had done a few minutes before.

But he of the scarred chin was of tougher courage. " It is not a difficult thing to mention a great name," he said, sneering and alert.

" I must teach you caution," said the magician, who, despite the goodness of his heart, could not bring himself to love these dark and bloodthirsty people. So, in a flash, he vanished from their sight. They uttered a shout of consternation, and the warrior with the sinister eyes and disfigured chin hurled his spear at the place where the stranger had stood. In the same instant of time he received a buffet on the head that laid him flat on the moss.

Black Eagle was soon brought to the magician, who now stood quietly, in his mild and visible form, calm as if nothing unusual had taken place. The chief greeted his visitor respectfully, for he knew him of old.

" Have you seen a man running on the air, as if he had the moccasins of the wind on his feet? " asked Wise-as-a-she-wolf.

" I saw such an one but two days ago. He was flying northward and westward, toward the Land of Giants," replied the chief of the mountaineers.

Wise-as-a-she-wolf continued his journey immediately, and soon came to the borders of that desolate region known as the Land of Giants. Its inhabitants were people of tremendous stature and physical strength. They were stupidly savage, and so dull of wit that no argument, save that of heavier clubs than their own, could move them. And as they had never met with heavier clubs than their own, no man could remember that their darkened opinions had ever been changed by outside influence. The biggest and strongest man was always their chief; and he remained their chief for just so long as he continued to be bigger and stronger than any of his people. When illness or old age weakened him then his chieftainship ended, and perhaps his life, into the bargain. Wise-as-a-she-wolf knew these people well, though not favourably; so he paused in his flight and descended to the ground at some distance from the first of the great lodges. Still invisible, he advanced cautiously on foot toward the untidy and tremendous structure of tree-trunks in which dwelt the giant who had been chief of the people at the time of his last visit to the country. He had not gone more than a dozen paces before he was halted by the sight of a human body, a lifeless body, lying face-downward on the moss and stones. At first he thought it was the body of one of the Mountain People; but, upon drawing nearer, he saw that the garments of dressed leather, blood-stained and wrinkled on that stiffened form, were of the pattern common among the warriors of his own country beyond the Narrow Sea. The feet were bare, but one of the moccasins lay close by. Very gently he turned the body over; and the face of the dead man was that of Spotted Seal, as Jumping Wolf had described it to him.

Wise-as-a-she-wolf turned away from the pitiful thing and went on in the direction of the great lodge, the shapeless roof of which loomed above a grove of spruces on the summit of a hill. At last he issued from the grove and stood in front of, and at a safe distance away from, the entrance to the giant's abode. This entrance was nearly half the height of the structure and wide in proportion. It looked more like the mouth of a den than the doorway of a human retreat. Bones of caribou and moose lay white on the trampled ground; but there was no sign of a cooking-fire to be seen. The giants ate their meat raw, and were never known to use fire even in winter, for the sake of its warmth. In the dusky interior, Wise-as-a-she-wolf detected the outline of a bulky figure.

CHAPTER XXII

WISE - AS - A - SHE - WOLF AND CRACK BONE THE GIANT

" Awake, chief, and come out from your den. Wise-as-a-she-wolf is here to talk to you," cried the magician, in a formidable voice.

The head and shoulders of the giant immediately appeared, and from under a fringe of tangled hair a pair of alert eyes, gray as ice, glared about on every side and up in the air. The giant's face was covered with untidy, yellow whiskers. His forehead sloped back sharply from his eyebrows, and his nose was flat. He crouched on all-fours, and in one massive hand, which rested on the ground, he grasped the smaller end of a trimmed pine tree. The magician thought of the littlest warrior, far away and alone in the magic lodge, and decided to act with discretion.

" Is it you, little great-man? " said the giant, in a voice that was not unlike the growling of a beast. " I don't see you," he continued. " Show yourself and come nearer. Old Crack Bone is ready to talk to you."

" I can talk to you very well from where I am," replied Wise-as-a-she-wolf. " All I want to know is, have you seen anything of two little red feathers? "

" I was afraid you had come to slay us all, mighty powerful one," said the giant, with a thunderous chuckle. " We might wade across to that little island of yours some day, and eat all your caribou and kill all your people," he added.

" And that will be time enough for me to slay you. Now I want you to give me the two red feathers which you took from the feet of the dead man," replied the magician.

" Was he one of your warriors? " asked the giant. " When I saw him flying along, like a bird, I thought it was the great Wise-as-a-she-wolf himself. So I just threw a little bone into the air, to attract his attention, and down he came, so hard that his life was knocked right out of him." Then he shook with horrible laughter at the re-membrance.

" Wise-as-a-she-wolf would never fly near you, without first making himself invisible. He knows you too well to trust you," replied the magician, sternly.

" The poor fellow whom you killed was not one of my people," he continued, " but the feathers are mine, for all that, and I must ask you to give them to me immediately."

" How can I give them to you, when I can't see you? " inquired the giant, with a grin.

" If you will kindly lay them on the top of your lodge," replied the other.

" Little great-one," said Crack Bone, " I am not afraid of you, or any magician, or anything alive under the sun. You can hide from my eye; but that does me no harm. As for the feathers, my brave warrior, why, I intend to keep them for my own use. They are of such virtue that, when I put them in my moccasins I can jump twice as high as my head. With a little more practice, I shall be able to fly as well as that unfortunate young man was flying before I tossed the shank-bone of a moose at him."

The magician was very angry at that, and felt a strong desire to increase his size and close in deadly combat with the giant. But he remembered the battle with Bright Robe, and the injuries then received, and thought of what might happen to the baby in the distant lodge if he should be disabled by the giant. So he changed his position, took a small stone from the ground, breathed upon it, and threw it into the roof of the giant's lodge. Next moment the whole structure was a mass of flames, and the giant, with a howl of rage, had scrambled from the dangerous place and hurled his club at where he thought the magician was standing. The huge weapon struck a clump of young spruce trees and broke them as if they were twigs; but the magician stood safe.

"Will you play any more of your magic on Crack Bone?" roared the giant, as he jumped again and again upon the fallen timber and threshed about with his club. Wise-as-a-she-wolf made no sound. Before Crack Bone had desisted from his violent dance, half a dozen of his people arrived on the scene, shouting questions and staring with amazement at the great pile of blazing timber that had so lately been the chief's lodge. At last Crack Bone leaned on his club, and, between gasps for breath (for the smoke from his burning den blew about him), answered some of their questions.

"It was that little magician, Wise-as-a-she-wolf,

from across the salt water," he said. " He came
for the red feathers. He told me to give him back
those fine red feathers. But he won't need them
now."

Crack Bone laughed victoriously, and drew the
tiny feathers from some safe hiding-place about his
person. He held them up, between his great
fingers, so that all might see. Then, bending
down, he slipped one into each of his moccasins.
The magician sprang high into the air, at sign of
these preparations, and hung at a safe distance
above the savage group, watchful but invisible.

" Stand aside, friends," roared Crack Bone.
" Now I have the magic feathers under my feet
and I intend to jump about, so don't stand too
close."

The other giants fell back the distance of a few
of their own great strides. Then Crack Bone
gathered himself together and leaped upward
with all the strength of his massive legs. Up he
shot, high above the surrounding tree-tops,
struggled in the air for a few seconds and sank
back to earth. The magic of the feathers was not
strong enough to keep his mountain-like body
afloat. His friends were greatly impressed by
this display of agility, and shouted until the earth

rang. But the magician, high and unseen, only smiled.

" I fear nothing," cried the giant, to his people. " Wise-as-a-she-wolf angered me, and now where is he? He set the red fire to eat my house to dust, but he was not strong enough to save his own life. Oh, I am strong and mighty, and have flying magic under my feet." At that he began to jump here and there, so recklessly that the other giants moved sullenly away.

" I think the feathers are safe in his keeping," said the magician. " He cannot harm my people with them, for they cannot lift so great a weight across the Narrow Sea. Some other time, when the littlest warrior is older and stronger, I shall return and win the feathers back. I shall always know where to find them."

With that, he set his face again in the direction of his own country and his own lodge, and flashed through the air with all the speed of the moccasins of the wind; and far behind and below, Crack Bone, the chief of the giants, continued to caper and shout before his blazing house.

Within a hundred yards of the giant, in the top of a fir tree, perched a little brown owl. He sat very still; but his yellow eyes were full of light and eagerness and cunning. He watched the stupid giant leaping and skipping on the magic feathers, and was glad that he had visited this desolate country.

CHAPTER XXIII

HOW CRACK BONE WAS DOUBLY OUTWITTED

THIS little brown owl that had been a spectator of the whole of Wise-as-a-she-wolf's interview with Crack Bone, and that now sat and watched the giant prancing victoriously, was none other than Bright Robe. He, too, believed that his enemy had been disabled by the giant's club and trodden to helplessness by the giant's feet. Otherwise, the magician would surely have replied to the giant's attack. One who could throw magic fire onto the roof of a lodge could as easily throw it against a man's body. But he knew that his enemy was not dead, however his body might be crushed and broken. He was aware that no mortal hand, either of giant or magician, could kill Wise-as-a-she-wolf.

The owl had crossed the Narrow Sea some time before Crack Bone's capture of the red feathers. He had visited the camps of the mountaineers, and the lodges of several magicians, and the caves of a fierce people still farther to the westward, and the lodges of the fat, blubber-eating people far to the northward; but, remembering his experiences in his own country, he had not made himself known to any one. He had practised the same discretion with the giants.

After the house was burned to the ground, Crack Bone strode up the hill and took possession of a lodge belonging to one of his people. The rightful owner was very angry, but he made no objections. He knew that he was no match for the chief, especially now that the chief was so light on his feet. The little owl followed Crack Bone, at a safe distance, watched him remove the feathers from his moccasins and tuck them under his belt, and then flew away to where some of the giants had thrown a number of fresh bones that were not entirely devoid of flesh. He ate his fill, keeping a sharp look-out all the while for foxes, and then returned to spy on the giant and the magic feathers.

Day after day the little brown owl kept watch over the actions of the chief of the giants. He followed the great savage on his hunting expeditions, watching him strike down moose and caribou and bear. In that desolate country summer was already past, and the owl was cold, for he had not yet made himself a winter retreat. The rivers and ponds froze and snow fell thick out of the gray skies; and still the owl followed Crack Bone or perched near his lodge, cold but determined. At last his alertness and watchfulness were rewarded. Crack Bone had been hunting and had used the red feathers, and the bird had followed him close, drifting from tree to tree. On reaching his lodge, Crack Bone immediately drew his moccasins from his feet and removed the feathers from them. It was now evening, and falling snow added to the gloom. The giant had killed three caribou; and just when in the act of hiding the feathers under his belt, he heard a sound of furtive movements near the spot where he had thrown the dead animals. He listened for a moment, then placed the feathers on a stone in the doorway of his lodge and sprang in the direction of the sound that had disturbed him. The owl fluttered to the ground, picked up the feathers in his beak, and flew away. He flew at his best speed, straight ahead through the gloom and the whirling snow. At last he alit in a great pine **tree** and hid the feathers in a crevice in the bark.

They would be safe there until morning. Then he snapped his beak and fluttered his wings. The red feathers were his, all ready to be placed in his moccasins when the enchantment was removed from him.

"I have done what Wise-as-a-she-wolf failed to do," he chuckled.

Crack Bone did not reach the place where he had left the carcasses of the caribou a moment too soon. Stone Hand, the giant whose house he had so unceremoniously taken, was turning away with all three of the bodies in his arms. Crack Bone struck at him with his fist; but Stone Hand avoided the blow by leaping to one side; and letting two of the frozen carcasses fall to the ground, he swung the other by the hind legs and smote the chief across the head with it. The blow staggered Crack Bone for a moment; but only for a moment. His skull was far too thick to be injured by any weapon so light and yielding as the body of a stag. He reeled a little, bellowed with anger, and clutched at Stone Hand. But he missed his mark in the swirling gloom, and the thief dashed away. Crack Bone stooped, lifted a great stone from the ground, and hurled it blindly after the mutinous one. Then, yanking a small tree from the frozen ground, to serve him as a club, he dashed into the storm and darkness in mad pursuit. Stone Hand turned sharply, and headed for the unpeopled wilds; but Crack Bone ran straight on, until he stumbled among the lodges of his people. They were upon him in a moment, striking blindly with all manner of weapons. Logs flew from the tops of the houses, and everybody hit at whatever was within reach. Crack Bone received some painful blows while he scrambled on all-fours. He got to his feet, and swung his improvised club recklessly but with great execution. Lodges and giants were overturned, in a horrible uproar that frightened the wild animals for miles around. Every one fought; but none knew what the fight was about or whom he fought with. All were fighting mad.

Stone Hand sat down and listened to the roars of combat from afar. " Since that old Crack Bone killed the magician and got hold of the jumping feathers," he said, " he thinks he is the master of the world. He took my fine, warm house away from me; and now I believe he has attacked the whole tribe."

He grunted and fell to devouring the one caribou that remained in his possession. He was hungry, for most of the game had moved southward since the coming of winter; and of late only Crack Bone, with the red feathers on his feet, had been able to overtake the herds. After eating the last bit of raw meat, Stone Hand lay down between two small hills and fell asleep. The snow span about him, and covered him from head to foot, as if he were a mountain. But he was full of food — that is, he had just enjoyed a moderate meal — so he slumbered soundly. For a long time the tumult of the distant battle continued to sift vaguely into his dreams.

The sun was above the horizon when Stone Hand opened his eyes. For a little while he wondered why he was not under cover, and stared stupidly at the hills on either side. He felt stiff and cold; but soon got to his feet and shook the snow from his limbs and body, and brushed it from his hair and face with his hands. Now he remembered how he had stolen the three caribou from the chief. He chuckled at the recollections of his escape and of the sounds of furious combat behind him. Now all was quiet, as if there had never been a shout, or the thump of a descending club, since the beginning of the world. He armed himself with a great piece of green timber and set out cautiously for the village, crawling on hands and knees. Now, in broad daylight, the familiar fear of the chief had returned to him. So he advanced slowly, and kept as close to the ground as he could. At last, peering over the top of a wooded hill, he obtained a clear view of the place which he had left so hurriedly the previous night. He gazed at the scene in amazement, for scarcely one of the lodges stood entire. Many were flat on the ground and the massive timbers and rocks of which they had been constructed lay scattered on all sides. Many others were unroofed. The surrounding trees were uprooted and broken, and the snow was trampled and stained with blood for hundreds of yards in every direction. And as for the inhabitants of this demolished village, — why, they seemed to be even in a worse way than their lodges. Some lay motionless on the snow, and others sat or reclined about their fallen homes, awkwardly dressing their wounds and groaning with pain. Not a giant of all that terrible company was able to stand on his feet.

As soon as an understanding of the true state of affairs got into Stone Hand's thick head, he stood upright and advanced fearlessly. He walked among his fallen tribesmen and grinned at them heartlessly. His glances rested on old Crack Bone, who sat with his head in his hands, and he looked both savage and jovial.

"I am your chief now," he said. "Does any one dispute my right?"

Groans were his only answer. Crack Bone did not so much as remove his hands from his head, which, I believe, he was doing his best to hold together.

"I am your chief," continued Stone Hand, "so I will go and hunt. If I kill more than I can eat myself I will give you some. But I must have the magic feathers on my feet, for the herds are far to the southward. Where are the feathers?" he asked, turning to Crack Bone.

The ex-chief groaned, and mumbled something to the effect that he neither knew nor cared.

"Give them to me," roared Stone Hand, angrily. "I am the chief now."

Then Crack Bone tried to explain, with many grunts and moans, that the feathers were not to be found; that he had laid them down on a stone in front of his lodge and that some one had stolen them during the fight. But, of course, the new and self-elected chief did not believe a word of it.

" Give them to me," he bellowed, swinging his club around the other's head. But Crack Bone sullenly persisted in his story of the loss of the magic feathers. So Stone Hand searched him, despite his cries and bellowings at the pain of it; and he did not find them.

The little owl, in the meantime, had discovered a deep hole, high up in a great birch tree. It was the deserted nest of a woodpecker. He dropped the feathers into the hole; and down they fell, quite out of his reach.

" They will be safe there," he said. " When I am ready to use them I will break the tree to splinters and take them out."

CHAPTER XXIV

THE MAGICIANS AWAKE

THE seasons passed, with melting snow, waning summers and scattering seeds. Many moons were born, each to grow and dwindle, and leave behind it in the blackness the germ of another moon. The herds of caribou moved southward and northward again, hunted by men and wolves, yet ever multiplying. The tribes grew; warriors did deeds of valour; death and pride and love moved among the lodges. Children were born; old people and strong hunters and little children set their feet on the Longest Trail. The north loosed its fields of ice in spring-time, freighted with cold and fogs and millions of seals; and so it had been since the beginning of things.

Run-all-day's village grew like the herds, and like the forests in the sheltered valleys, until it became a great clan. Run-all-day had lost nothing of his authority with the loss of the magic feathers, for his people loved him. He was the head-chief of the clan, and under him were four lesser chiefs, among whom was Jumping Wolf, the young warrior from the south. And Jumping Wolf had a lodge of his own, and Singing Bird was his wife.

Wise-as-a-she-wolf kept close to his magic house, for it seemed that his whole heart was with the littlest warrior. He named the child Feather-foot, for the magic feathers were to be his, and his alone, as soon as they were won back from Crack Bone, the giant. But the magician seemed to be in no haste to make that long journey again. There would be plenty of time for it later; and now he had so many things to teach the child. Little Featherfoot learned readily, for he grew, both in brain and body, at twice the rate of an ordinary child. And so, when he was in his sixth summer, he was as large as a boy of twelve summers, and knew magic that was beyond the understanding of any save the great magicians. He could make fire in a moment, even as Wise-as-a-she-wolf had done to burn the lodge of Crack Bone. His bow would send an arrow the distance of six flights of an ordinary arrow, and no weapon, unless it were tipped with magic, could break or pierce his shield of thin leather. He could take upon himself the semblance of a wolf, a caribou, or a bear, and at such times his speed was as the speed of the former animals and his strength as that of the latter. Also, he could make light objects heavy, and heavy objects as light as birch bark.

While Bright Robe hid in desolate places, harmless but expectant, and the good magician sat in his lodge, and Run-all-day's people prospered and grew, men were blowing on red coals in almost every camp and village in the island. And the coals they blew upon were the memories of old battles, and they were red with the fires of old hatreds. The fires leaped up and touched their flames to the hearts of the warriors. The tribes had been too long at peace with one another. In the south, and the east, and the west, they made their war-arrows; and the lonely hunters and fishers of the north heard of it and returned to their villages, with the lust of fighting in their hearts. And Run-all-day felt the stirring of the trouble in the air, and armed his men, and sent swift and cunning messengers to spy upon the other clans.

" I was once a peaceful hunter and fisher," said he, to Red Willow, " but now I am the chief of a people. If the men of other villages come against me, then must I do battle with them, to the best of my ability. It is stupid to fight without cause; but it is better to fight, and give back blows for every one received, than to crouch in one's lodge and die like a frightened hare."

Being but a man, after all, he prayed in his heart that his master, the good magician, would not pacify the tribes until he had proved his little army. There was fighting blood in him; and a flame of that red coal that had lain ash-hidden for so long a time, had got into his honest heart.

Wise-as-a-she-wolf told Featherfoot the story of the red feathers; and about two months before the time that Bright Robe would return to his old form and power, he set out for the land of the giants, armed with magic weapons, to bring Crack Bone to terms. But Crack Bone was dead and Stone Hand ruled in his place. When the magician asked word of the feathers, the true story of the fight and of their sudden disappearance was told to him, first by Stone Hand and afterward by several others of the giants. Wise-as-a-she-wolf was disturbed at the news, and blamed himself for not having taken the feathers from Crack Bone long ago. Also, he knew nothing of the whereabouts of Bright Robe, and this, too, disturbed the peace of his mind. He set to work immediately to find the red feathers. He hunted far and wide, questioning the people of many tribes. He went north, to the farthest village, and southward to the great wooded countries, where are thousands of red-skinned people, and fields of corn, and trees bearing fruits. But nowhere did he hear any word of the red feathers. For the space of two moons he sought the lost treasures; but at last he turned homeward, and ran upon the air, with all the speed of the moccasins of the wind, for a day and a night and a day. When he came to the western coast of his own country, he saw below him, lying black and lifeless, the ruins of a village. Then he knew that the tribes were at war again; and again he blamed himself for having neglected his duties toward his people. He descended to the ground and saw the bodies of men, with wounds upon them, and broken weapons.

Bright Robe, in the meantime, was tasting the joy of his old ways again. The moment he had returned to his old shape, he had increased his man-strength an hundred times and splintered the pine tree. Then he had placed the feathers in his moccasins and crossed the Narrow Sea. Again

he was the master of his magic; and though he had
lost the silver robe that had turned him invisible
at will, the newly acquired feathers more than
made up for the loss. But he had learned discretion during his five summers spent in the shape
of an owl, and so was content to go quietly among
the islanders for a little while, making no demonstrations of his power. He even concealed his
identity and avoided the lodges of people who
knew him. He made himself agreeable by many
fires, talked modestly, and listened attentively
to the words of old men and warriors. And so he
learned that his enemy, Wise-as-a-she-wolf, had
been very quiet of late, and that all the clans were
uneasy with war-lust. He knew that the power
of Wise-as-a-she-wolf would suffer if the people
fought, for those who suffered would feel that he
had withdrawn his protection from them, and
those who conquered would know that they had
done so without any help from him. Therefore
he was anxious to see the islanders battling among
themselves, and after considering the matter,
and investigating the relative strengths of the
larger clans and their leaders, he disclosed himself to the chief of the people of a great district
in the south. This chief was a veritable king,

with four villages and hundreds of miles of hunting country under his rule. His name was Cold Wind, and his heart was harder than the ice-fields of the north. So to him Bright Robe made himself known, and offered to give him assistance in the battle and at the council fire.

Cold Wind dared not refuse Bright Robe's offer; but he was not pleased at having a greater person than himself on the scene. The warriors were called together, armed for battle, and the campaign was begun with the destruction of that village in which lived the old woman called Hot Tongue, and those great warriors, Yellow Fox, Seven Knives, Strong Hunter, and Mighty Hand. Bright Robe had no pleasant memories of that village; so the people were slain, and the lodges robbed of their treasures of fur and food and then burned to the ground. The victorious fighting-parties travelled westward then and destroyed many little villages. But the clans rose on every side to stem the course of Cold Wind's people; so Bright Robe retired from the scene of action, knowing that the mischief was well begun.

Bright Robe did not want to attract Wise-as-a-she-wolf's attention again, for he knew that he was neither strong nor cunning enough to withstand that great magician. So he left Cold Wind and the warriors, and crossed the island, to continue quietly in his evil ways. And at every village and every camp he questioned the people concerning his enemy's whereabouts and affairs. The people had heard nothing of the great magician for several seasons, so Bright Robe learned nothing by his questionings. He began to believe and hope that Wise-as-a-she-wolf had left the country.

Wise-as-a-she-wolf returned to his lodge and told Featherfoot of his journey, and of its fruitlessness. Of this matter, and of the signs of warfare which he had beheld in the west, he spoke at length. The child was eager to go in search of the feathers, but of that the magician would not hear.

" May I help my people in the fighting? " he asked. " With my magic, I am already stronger than any warrior, and with my shield I can turn aside the heaviest and swiftest arrow. I have no fear, master, and yet I know the value of caution. With the knowledge that you have taught me, even now I would be a help to my people."

" Nay," cried the good magician, sorely troubled. " Nay, you are still but a child at heart, for all your size and strength. Your hand would stay in the stroke, for very pity, even when your life was at risk. Keep the protection of this lodge, and I am your friend. Your people shall be under my special protection until such time as I can show the clans the foolishness of this strife among themselves."

It was for love of this child that Wise-as-a-she-wolf had postponed the contest with the giant, and by that had lost the magic feathers; and now, for the father-love in his heart, he wanted to keep the child in the safety of the lodge, where the very powers that he had given him were of no use to mankind.

CHAPTER XXV

THE UNFINISHED BATTLE

RUN-ALL-DAY's fighting force consisted of about one hundred and forty warriors, well armed and trained. Every man of them could shoot straight and strong with the bow, and throw his club and spear with accuracy and force. All had strong shields with which to guard their bodies, and blades of flint in their belts for use in hand-to-hand grapplings. There were scouts lurking afar, to the south and west, — swift runners to bring word to the village of the trend and progress of the different battles and war-parties. The village was enclosed in a breast-high fence of brush and tree-trunks, and the warriors kept within easy reach of the lodges, ready to answer a call to arms at any time of the day or night.

It was early of a June morning when two runners entered the village gasping for breath, and told the chief that they had seen several war-parties at a distance of about four hours' journey to the southward. They had found them at night, asleep around small fires, and were not certain of their numbers. They were lying on the ground close as the stones in the bed of a river, each rolled in his sleeping-robe and looking very long and broad in the uncertain light. Run-all-day called the lesser chiefs and most experienced warriors into his lodge, and a council of war was held without delay. Jumping Wolf volunteered to set out immediately, with a small party of the swiftest among the young men, to spy upon the approaching enemy and return with word of their strength.

" It is a good plan," said Run-all-day; and the others nodded their heads. So Jumping Wolf selected six youths to accompany him, and left the village. They carried no arms save the knives in their belts; but their shields, spears, and clubs were to be held in readiness against their return.

When Jumping Wolf had been gone an hour, the council's plans were settled. A chief named Tall Pine advanced into the hilly, wooded country to the southward, close along the eastern shore of the stream, with thirty men. His orders were to halt and take cover a mile from the village, throwing his men in a thin line across the probable course of the enemy. This line was to let the

leading body of the enemy pass through it, and
then close in, on the flanks of the invaders, with
fire of arrows and spears. Another force of thirty
warriors, with a chief named Red Sky in command,
took position a few hundred yards in rear of the
other, where the river begins to widen into the
bay, and spread from the rocks of the coast across
the front of the village. This party was to strike
the enemy in front, at the first sounds of conflict.
Both these parties were to fall back upon the
main body, after loosing a few volleys and striking
a few swift blows. The main body, consisting of
over seventy men, and led by Run-all-day and
several other chiefs, lay in close ranks in front of
the village, well hidden among rocks and brush.

It was about three hours before noon when
Jumping Wolf's party returned from the scouting
and joined the advance line, where their arms
and shields were awaiting them. They had run far
and fast, had seen the enemy advancing in three
lines, and had returned at top speed. Jumping
Wolf reported the number of the enemy as close
upon three hundred. A fresh runner was sent
back with the information, and the scouts remained with Tall Pine.

An hour passed — two hours passed — and

still the wilderness lay quiet under the warm and high-wheeling sun. Jumping Wolf crawled away from the line of impatient warriors and slipped into the rugged places. He was soon back again, and crouched beside Tall Pine.

" They are within bow-shot's distance," he whispered. " The leading party will touch that open hillside," and he pointed with his finger.

The word went along the line, and every concealed warrior fixed his gaze on the rocky slope indicated, and set the notches of arrows to the taut strings. The figure of a man appeared suddenly from the scrubby growth above the clearing. He stood upright and gazed ahead, and on every side, under a shading hand. At last, evidently satisfied with the result of his survey, he waved his arm and advanced further into the open. He stooped, and took advantage of every bit of cover, moving swiftly forward all the while. They came after him quickly and noiselessly, every man following the tactics of the leader in crossing the open space. The party numbered more than seventy warriors. Upon reaching the foot of the slope, where the ground was rough and lightly wooded, they closed in an irregular formation and increased their speed.

They seemed to be in a great hurry to add one more smoking village to the list of their military achievements. They hastened along, four and five abreast, close-ranked, lulled to carelessness by the ease of former victories.

The twanging of bow-strings opened the battle-music, and the arrows swished and struck. The invaders scattered, and sprang to right and left in search of Tall Pine's hidden warriors; and from either side the arrows continued to leap from rock and bush and tree. The long shafts rattled across the shields and stood deep in flesh and muscle; and even while the invaders dashed here and there, Red Sky appeared in front of them, with his thirty men, and advanced swiftly behind a shower of arrows. The leader of the enemy rallied his scattered fighters and led them against the new arrivals; but only forty of his seventy were able to join the charge. Red Sky met them with a flight of spears; and at the same moment the bow-men under Tall Pine and Jumping Wolf sprang into sight and closed upon their rear.

Soon the victors were busy collecting arrows, drawing them from dead bodies and gathering them up from the ground. A few had wounds to bind, but only a few. It had been a swift and

easy victory for the skirmishers of Run-all-day's
army, and not more than a dozen of the invaders
had escaped death by flight.

Suddenly more of the enemy issued from the
woods above the open hillside, and rushed down
the slope, score after score. It was the main body,
numbering more than two hundred fighting-men.
They came at their best pace, wondering, no
doubt, why the sounds of combat had ceased;
perhaps believing that Run-all-day was already
overthrown, and in haste to join in the looting
of the village. By the time the scene of the
fight was reached, only the dead awaited
them.

The sixty victors fell noiselessly back and joined
the double line of defenders in front of the village.
Word of the brief fight and of the approach of the
main body of the enemy passed from mouth to
mouth. Then all lay still, close to the ground,
and breathlessly awaited the arrival of the invaders. They had a fairly clear view of the land
for several hundred yards in front of their coverts.
At last the vanguard of the enemy appeared
among the little hummocks and clumps of trees,
and a great shout went up from them at the sight
of what appeared to them an unprotected village.

Of what account is a barrier of brush if there are no warriors to strengthen it?

Then, standing upright between the hidden defenders and the invaders swiftly forming line for attack, appeared the figure of a young man in garments of dressed leather, richly decorated. The advance was halted, and the warriors of Run-all-day held their arrows.

" Go back to your villages," cried the young man to the southerners. " You have shed too much blood of your own countrymen. Turn on your trail of blood and ashes, and go back to your deserted lodges."

" It is the good magician. It is Wise-as-a-she-wolf," whispered Run-all-day's warriors.

" Who speaks so mightily? " cried a young chief from the ranks in front. " Are we to be turned back by a voice, who have scattered the people of ten encampments? " and he bent his bow.

" Yes! Though the voice has been silent over-long," replied the magician. " Unstring your bows, and return to your own lands, and mourn the ruin you have done."

At that the young chief raised his bow.

" Loose the arrow, fool," cried the other; and

the arrow flew. And he extended his hand and plucked it from the air and dropped it, harmless, to the ground.

"I am Wise-as-a-she-wolf, whom men once called Highest Star," said the magician. "Is this your gratitude for a hundred seasons of protection?"

"Let us at them, master," cried Run-all-day, springing to his feet.

The magician halted and silenced the great chief with a gesture of his hand. Then he advanced upon the wavering southerners who lusted for blood and the treasures of the village in spite of the fear in their hearts.

"All the people of this island are my people, else would I strike you for your sins of greed and blood-thirstiness," said Wise-as-a-she-wolf, walking steadily forward.

"The master is angry. I hear it in his voice. He will strike them in his wrath," whispered Run-all-day to a man beside him.

True, the magician was angry, for all the gentleness of him; and the anger shone in his eyes, and scattered the men of the south before him. They ran to right and left, but they did not turn back toward their own villages. And the young chief

who had loosed the arrow, called the more daring
of his followers to stand firm. So wicked was his
heart, and so full was it of vanity, that he knew
nothing of discretion. He hurled two spears, in
quick succession, at the good magician.

Wise-as-a-she-wolf snatched the spears from the
air, stood for a second with one in either hand,
and then vanished from the sight of friend and
foe. Next moment the arrogant young chief lay
dead on the ground, struck down by an invisible
weapon. At that, the invaders turned and ran
southward, frantic with terror, each warrior expecting immediate death from the unseen hand.
Wise-as-a-she-wolf knew that their hearts were
hard, and that their lesson was not yet learned,
so he ordered Run-all-day and his warriors to
follow the fugitives and deliver six flights of
arrows.

Not more than half of the three hundred
southern warriors got safely back to their own
country; and they were spent and sore, and full
of regret for their misdeeds. Also, they were
none the richer for their great campaign, for
they had retreated so whole-heartedly from Run-
all-day's village, that they had thrown away
their spoils of former victories to lighten their